THE BODY BIZ

The Pilates Story

Joan Breibart

PMI PUBLISHERS
NEW YORK

The Body Biz
PMI Publishers
84 Wooster Street NY NY 10012
www.themethodpilates.com
www.dietdirectives.com

Copyright 2006 © by Joan Breibart
All rights reserved

Cover by Kay Sherdian
Design by James Sheehan

Library of Congress Cataloging in Publication Data:

Breibart, Joan
Body Biz, The
p. cm
ISBN: 1-4243-1677-4
1. Fiction
Printed in the United States of America

ISBN: 1-4243-1677-4

For Doug, Peter, and Roger

ACKNOWLEDGEMENTS
Cathy Hannan, Meredith Luce, and Marika Molnar
for their support through the years

THANKS TO
Lauren McLaughlin, Kay Sheridan, Anne Sommers, Joan Arnold,
and Cessarina Ferro for their advice and assistance

CONTENTS

THE BODY BIZ

PILATES CHRONIOLOGY
1880 - 2006

1880   Joseph H. Pilates born: creator, Pilates Method
         of Contrology

1912   Joseph is interned as a German Nationalist

1920   Joe meets Clara, they arrive in America and marry

1925   Frederick Pilates makes first Reformers

1925   The Pilates Studio opens at 939 8th Avenue NYC

1964   Weight Watchers Inc. starts diet business

1965   Henri Bendel's Pilates Studio opens

1967   Joseph H. Pilates dies

1968   Eve Gentry opens Pilates Studio in Santa Fe, NM

1969   Clara Pilates stops teaching

1969   Romana Kryzanowska heads Pilates studio

1970   The Pilates Studio moves to 29 West 56th NYC

1970   Alan Herdman opens London Pilates studio

1971   Ron Fletcher's Pilates Studio opens in LA

1975   Pilates taught at State University of New York

1975   Current Concepts (Balanced Body) begins
         apparatus manufacturing

1980   Pilates Studio changes ownership
                 Aris Isotoner   1984-1986
                 Healite 1986-1988

1988   Pilates Studio closes

1991   *Institute for the Pilates Method* (Pilates Institute) opens

1992   Sean Gallagher brings first court actions
         against Pilates instructors

1994   Sean Gallagher sues Pilates Institute for trademark infringement

1994   Eve Gentry dies in Santa Fe, NM

1996   Sean Gallagher sues Balanced Body (BB)

2000   TM suit goes to trial. Victory for BB on October 19. Pilates mark is declared generic. Equipment and exercise instruction marks are declared invalid from abandonment, registration fraud or invalid assignment.

2002   **PhysicalMind Institute** moves to NYC

2003   Nine million people in the US practice Pilates

2004   **Diet Directives** site is launched

2005   Weight Watchers sales reach $1.3 billion

2005   Sixty-three percent of health clubs offer Pilates

2006   11 million people in the U.S practice Pilates

2006   The Pilates Chair is launched at IDEA fitness show

PROLOGUE

1988

"In America....only he (Saul Steinberg) could have dreamed up the poster that summarizes the Manhattanite's provincial view of America: Ninth and Tenth Avenues wide in the foreground, a strip of Hudson River, a smaller strip of New Jersey, and in the background a few scattered cities—Los Angeles, Las Vegas, Chicago—with Japan and China in the distance."
—**Time Magazine, 1978**

"Y ou're moving to Santa Fe? That's crazy. I know you. The first week there you'll unpack, decorate, landscape, and acquire a Southwestern wardrobe. What will you do the second week?" Johanna's friend Mark Salters, the New York chef/author of the moment, shouted in disbelief.

Mark wasn't saying anything Johanna hadn't thought herself, multiple times. Actually, though, they were both only half right. Johanna's persona confused most people, even those who knew her well. One of the things that they didn't get about her was that she truly loved, was at her most serene, in exquisite natural settings. The other half of this equation, what did, however, give her terrific pause, was the prospect of assimilating herself into the real America. With her DNA, she could never become mellow, lackadaisical, slow talking or slow moving. It was biologically a problem. For her husband Dan, though, continuing to live a caffeinated New York existence could prove fatal. He just couldn't take it anymore, but that was their secret.

"Oh come on. We're going to relax, luxuriate in the sun. Absorb the scenery. Play tennis and ski. Enjoy the Opera, and learn about Indian culture. We'll become part of the Canyon Road Art scene, which has dozens of galleries. It's like Soho with parking.

"Who needs to work 80 hours a week?" Johanna added, a little defensively even though she appreciated Mark's outburst. It showed that he cared about her welfare.

"And what does our good friend Meredith have to say about this Wild West adventure?"

"She thinks it will probably be a little slow paced for me, but she feels Dan could benefit from a break."

"A break, sure. Take a long vacation. Just don't burn any bridges, don't sell your apartment or your country house. Selling your real estate, it's like taking a one-way ticket."

"But not for us, because if we decide to come back we won't need such a big apartment. Phillip starts college next year and Ross will be gone in three years, too."

"Speaking of your terrific sons, what's their take on

heading out West?"

"For them, it's like exchanging vacations at the Massachusetts barn for vacations at a ski lodge near Taos. Remember that Ross is at boarding school, when it's open that is. You've heard my litany on the subject of schools: half a day, half a year. Summer vacation is three and a half months. Christmas begins at Thanksgiving. For this we pay twenty grand plus housing. And, on the subject of housing, Manhattanites' favorite topic of conversation, the prices in Santa Fe are half of what we shell out here for shelter, which means 50 percent less stress."

"Okay. I see where this is going. Let me guess: quality of life? But what about the quality of people, the energy they give off? Sorry Johanna, I just don't see you in a tiered skirt sipping herbal tea out of a paper cup. You're never, ever, going to fit in with the New Age types. When they start extolling the virtues of tree hugging, granola, and spirituality, you will not be able to just nod and smile politely like most people would. You'll tell them exactly how you see it; you're incapable of censoring yourself just to get along."

Mark was right, but uncharacteristically, she wouldn't tell him so. "When you visit, I'm sure I'll be able to round up some espresso cups and a few civilized, cynical, easily bored, worldly types for you to hang with."

"Right. And remember to send me a shopping list of all the things they don't have there, like arugula, goat cheese, milk fed veal, paté, calamari ... I'll probably have to drive out there in a refrigerated truck because no airline would ever let me bring that much stuff. By the way, will a visa be necessary?"

"This conversation is proof that New Yorkers are certified xenophobes."

"And that's why you're the consummate New Yorker and should never leave. And what about that weird exercise thing you're pushing like it's a religion. I bet you won't find that out there on the prairie."

"Santa Fe is in the mountains, Mark," she mock lectured. "It's 7,000 feet above sea level. And yes, when it comes to Pilates, I'm really going to miss it. It's been incredibly good for me. But I can't put my life on hold because I've bonded with a Reformer. You know my departure could prove to be quite an opportunity for you."

"Because I could start a catering business there in New Mexico?"

She drilled him with a 'be serious' look. "No, because my time slot at the Pilates studio will open up. I'm sure I can arrange to transfer it to you, just don't tell anyone else. We like to keep this anti-aging secret within our tribe."

After Mark left, Johanna allowed herself a brief moment to experience trepidation over the move, to acknowledge all she was leaving behind. After all, she was living the Town & Country lifestyle people salivated for. A big loft in a premier West Side co-op. Views of the Hudson River from sixteen oversized windows, just like living on a yacht moored on the 17th floor. Weekends at their renovated barn in Massachusetts. Membership in the best Westchester tennis and golf club. The right private schools. Staff. Glam jobs with expense accounts, business travel. Dinners at highly starred restaurants. Theatre, ballet, invitations. Best friends.

Johanna knew that finding new friends, even acquaintances, was the big unknown. Surely they would join a club so there would be invitations. They could build a social life. Her best friends, however, would remain here, thousands of miles away.

Johanna's musings did not indicate she was having doubts about their decision to move. No second-guessing. She was superb at making decisions, the best. Contemplation over, she would book the flight that would take her two thousand miles from home. First class, of course.

Part 1
The Early Years 1991-1994

"*However many fitness professionals—including those at the Aerobics Center, Tom Landry Sports Medicine And Research Center, the American Physical Therapy Association and IDEA, the Association for Fitness Professionals—say they are unfamiliar with Pilates. That may be because until July 1991, when the **Institute for the Pilates Method** was founded, there was no organization to promote the method, train instructors and otherwise get the word out.*"

*—**The Dallas Morning News, 1992***

1

LEE

"It's called the Pilates Method, but this exercise isn't some kind of torture from biblical times. While it involves odd-looking contraptions, Pontius Pilate doesn't enter into it at all."

—The Vancouver Sun, 1992

"**S**o this Lee Raney is Mac proficient, knows Quark, and has graphic experience. Sounds like we should interview her. You understand we are not looking for an artist. There's running the office, too. It's not all creative," Johanna half warned, half explained to Maria Theresa, the headhunter at New Vistas Employment.

"Pee-latz is close, but the name is pronounced Puh-lah-teez. Just tell her that we are a publishing and training organization. Thirty-Three Palace. The name's on the door. We'll both interview her so she should plan on an hour at least. Tell her to ask for Margaret. She's my business partner and in charge of teacher training. Thanks, Maria. She sounds terrific."

Johanna was exhausted from vocalizing. She had made or fielded five telephone calls already that morning and was certain she had spelled and pronounced Pilates several times during each conversation. Peelotz, Pilots, Pillatz. Maybe it wasn't too late to change the name of the Institute.

Or, maybe she should have a tape made that would be required listening for people who wanted to talk to her about Pilates: *Everything You Wanted To Know About Pilates But Didn't Know Whom To Ask*. Tape first. Johanna second.

> *Pilates is a Greek name, but Joseph Pilates came here from Germany. It is a body conditioning system, meaning exercise for thinking people. It's anaerobic, not aerobic. And it has nothing, absolutely nothing, to do with Pontius Pilate.*

Margaret could do the audio; she still spoke too quickly for the people out here. Instead of playing music for on-hold callers, they could play the tape. A definite win-win. Callers would no longer embarrass themselves mispronouncing Pilates, and she could save her voice because she would no longer have to begin each call with a spelling lesson.

# # # # #

Lying on the *banco* in her bedroom in paint encrusted jeans, inhaling blue corn chips and salsa, the phone jammed between her shoulder and ear, Lee Raney listened again to Maria Theresa's message. Uh, Lee thought.

Did she say peelatz institute? Something like that? Doesn't matter, she decided. It's a job, with a new business, and they might want someone permanently who can do graphic design. And, the office was near Sena Plaza, her favorite part of town. Perfecto. Peelatz. Whatever.

Lee found living in Santa Fe easy, but paying for it was something else. Aside from thousands of realtors, there's probably one under every Pinon tree, actual careers required a law degree or an understanding of cold fusion. Like other tourists before her, Lee had ventured to 'the land of enchantment' and discovered that she didn't want to leave. After dropping out of art school in gray and gloomy Boston, she blended right into the local art scene. While she scored lots of temp office gigs and infrequent design jobs, she was still short of cash. But, at least she had time to paint. In her seven years there, she'd never really had a chance to convert a temp position to a real job. This could be the one.

She dug out her official interview uniform—a white tunic, long denim skirt, and more silver jewelry than anyone in Boston would wear in a year, relieved that her garb camouflaged those extra thirty she'd put on from her green chile cheese burrito addiction. Drawing her brown hair back into a ponytail, she added some sunscreen and lip-gloss. She would charm these peelats people, whomever they were. She wondered if peelatz translated to "pilots". Managing an office and doing graphics for a bunch of pilots wouldn't be so bad.

La Sena Plaza's long portal fronted onto Palace Avenue, hiding from the street her favorite courtyard. Withe no time to dawdle, she kept up her pace and arrived at Thirty Three Palace, a two story territorial building sandwiched between a pricey leather goods store and her prior secretarial employment. On the door was a small metal plaque: **Pilates Institute**. Though her Spanish was coming along, she'd never seen the word Pilates before.

The door, in typical Santa Fe mode, was unlocked and open. She stepped inside to a darkish room, lined with mirrors. Lee could just make out three odd shaped platforms. Two looked like futon frames, the third appeared to be an oversized massage table with vertical metal poles growing from each corner. Various straps and springs added to her sense of strange. Giant rubber balls and a half dozen blue spongy mats lined the walls. Lee tried to imagine what anyone, let alone pilots, would be doing with such contraptions.

"Hello?" she said to no one.

Up above she heard movement, then the sound of feet coming down a flight of stairs. A very tall and toned woman, maybe five ten, with short, boyish hair, appeared, stepped forward and extended her hand.

"You must be Lee," she said. "I'm Margaret Holmes."

Lee fumbled awkwardly as she reached for Margaret's fingertips.

"Hi," she said. "Lee Ramey, from..."

"...New Vistas," Margaret said. "Yes. Thank you for coming."

The smile she gave Lee registered as automatic, robotic. Turning away, she glided to the windows and opened one of the wooden blinds to let in the sunshine. There was something about the way she moved. Her back was incredibly erect and her head was centered perfectly above her perfect shoulders. She made straightening up a stack of cushions an expression of grace.

"I see that you have never been to a Pilates studio before," Margaret said, when she caught Lee's expression.

Though Margaret was subtle, Lee caught her eyes drifting up and down her body. From Margaret's once over, Lee knew it wasn't just her unfamiliarity with the contraptions that made her alien. Sucking in, she tried to flatten her stomach.

"What are Pilotes?" Lee asked

The corners of Margaret's eyes wrinkled as she laughed gently, not too mockingly.

"Is Pulaatees," she enunciated every syllable. "What is Pilates."

Lee's fingers drifted nervously to her turquoise cross. "Sorry," Lee said.

"Don't be. Shall we go upstairs and I'll show you the office."

Margaret led them upstairs and into a small room brightly lit by a skylight through which the branches of a familiar Aspen were just visible. A long Mission wood table, two matching hard-backed chairs, a Macintosh computer on a small Mexican-style blue painted table, another giant ball and a life-sized skeleton attached to a wooden base were crowded into the small space. Anatomy diagrams and framed photos covered the walls. One photo showed a stocky man wearing only shorts doing poses on a box, and another, several women in old-fashioned leotards posing in bizarre configurations on frames like the ones downstairs.

Completing the wall montage was a framed news clipping entitled: *"They All Go to Joe's."* Looking closer, Lee discovered that Joe was Joe Pilates. Huh, so Pilates is not a thing, but a man, she thought to herself as Margaret moved a chair and motioned for her to sit in it. Lee sat down self-consciously, feeling clumsy and squat. Margaret towered above her: regal and very imposing. Mutt and Jeff, Lee thought.

"I have a client in a few minutes,"Margaret told her.

"When Johanna arrives, she can explain to you in detail our structure and our mission."

"Okay," Lee said wondering why Margaret couldn't just tell her.

Margaret pulled the giant ball closer and sat on it folding her endless legs in Indian position. "Now then," she said. "Of course we'll be needing general support in the office, and help with the correspondence and the telephone."

Her voice was elegant, measured, each word—no each syllable—pronounced with exact articulation. She spoke slowly and paused often to smile and make sure Lee was taking it all in. Lee, straining to match Margaret's posture vertebrae by vertebrae, was doing her best to straighten up and listen.

"There will be filing, maintaining mailing lists and very soon we'd like to begin the creation of a database. I understand you know how to operate one of those."

She let her eyes wander to the lone Mac.

"The computer?" Lee said.

Margaret nodded, engaging only her head in a

tiny movement.

"Yess," Lee said, over-pronouncing the S to match Margaret's enunciation.

"Very good," she smiled. "Since the first assignment is the design of the Reformer Encyclopedia."

I'm going to design an encyclopedia? Lee thought. Great. I'll definitely be here awhile.

Margaret unfolded herself and glided over to a file cabinet somewhat hidden behind a Segura cactus in the corner. She pulled out a thick manila file folder and handed it to Lee.

"This is what we have so far," she said. "Obviously, we'll be adding to it."

She returned to the Mission table and elegantly lifted herself onto it. "It is the first of its kind," she said from her perch.

"We're very excited."

Lee looked up at Margaret who appeared now like a preying mantis looking down on her. If Margaret was excited, she hid it well. Everything about Margaret's patrician persona unnerved her. Lee still had no idea what Pilates was, other than a man named Joe who wore skimpy shorts. What's a reformer? Should she know? Perhaps everyone knew.

The door opened downstairs and a woman's voice called up. "Hello?"

"We're up here, Eve," Margaret called down, then to Lee "That will be Ms. Gentry. Believe it or not, she was Joe's first teacher trainee and she's been a teacher herself for 45 years."

She heard footsteps ascending the stairs. Then a very tiny woman, barely five feet tall, appeared wearing a paisley outfit, almost a costume, with long bell-like sleeves and flowing pants. Her face said she was probably seventy, but she moved like a much younger woman. Matching Margaret's easy fluidity, she too glided rather than walked. She extended a papery hand toward Lee who rose to shake it.

She smiled warmly; her face was still beautiful. While Eve seemed more sincerely welcoming than Margaret, her posture was equally perfect, so Lee continued to stand like a private being introduced to sergeants, sergeants who might never say 'at ease, men.'

Eve opened a black leather appointment book and

read aloudthe entry. "Tom Forsythe today at three," she announced then turned to Lee, "ACL repair. Running. Overuse injuries are so common now. Joe always knew about the problems with repetitive movements. And they never listened."

Lee smiled nervously feeling like the dumbest person in the world. What did ACL stand for? Were these women some kind of New Age nurses without uniforms? And what about those S & M machines downstairs?

"So pleasant to meet you, Lee."

She retreated back down the stairs, but not without casting a quick up and down glance at Lee's body. Lee was trying so hard to keep her shoulders back she was afraid a rib would crack.

Shit, these people are so into bodies.

"I learned everything I know from Eve," Margaret said. "Studying with her for years: observing, practicing, and then finally apprenticing. Up until now, meaning as we speak, that's the way Pilates was practiced and passed on. You found someone through word of mouth and you hoped what she was teaching you was truly Pilates. We're going to change all that. We're designing a curriculum for a formal teaching program and graduates will be certified teachers. It's a very daunting project."

"I bet," Lee concurred.

"The Institute itself was originally Johanna's idea. It's only three months old." She glanced at the slim black watch on her wrist. "You'll meet her soon." She laughed her unsettling gentle laugh again. "Be prepared, she is likely to overwhelm you."

Lee nodded and smiled nervously. What a weird job interview, she thought.

"Johanna is a big thinker," Margaret continued. "A very, very big thinker. She wants to—she made quotation signs with her fingers—'put Pilates on the map.' She's passionate about Pilates and thinks it's on the brink of becoming the next big trend. Eve and I have been doing this for a long time and it's hard for us to believe, but we don't know anything about business. We're dancers—former dancers, of course."

Lee nodded, the picture growing less clear. Truthfully, she still had no idea what Margaret was talking about, but all she'd managed to do in the last three months was get dumped by her boyfriend, get laid off from another secretarial job, and increase her credit card debt by $647.42.

"Well," Margaret said. "That's Johanna for you. She has two speeds—fast forward and collapse. We haven't seen collapse yet."

She expanded her laugh repertoire, and sounded a tight, formal laugh.

The door opened downstairs and she heard Eve's voice and that of another woman.

Margaret floated down from the table, as if to begin a pirouette. "Very good," she said. "Johanna can continue." She extended her hand towards Lee as if awaiting Baryshnikov to take it. "A pleasure to meet you, Lee."

Lee met her fingertips with hers and gripped ever so gently.

"Likewise," she said.

After a staccato of footsteps, a fashion plate in her mid-thirties appeared in the office, somewhat breathless. She was slender, small boned with shoulder length auburn hair and perfect skin. Wearing Chanel No. 5, a charcoal linen sheath dress, and three-inch patent leather sling backs, she looked like a page out of *Vogue*. She dropped a black leather shoulder bag with an aggressive designer logo onto the table. After twenty years in Boston, Lee knew she could beam up the designer if she tried. Probably Prada.

Johanna extended her manicured hand. Her handshake was assertive. "Hello. How are you. You know Quark, right?"

"I do," Lee said.

"Good, you'll need it. Margaret, Lee and I are going to walk over to Santa Fe Subscription and pick up an article Meredith told me about," she said.

"Glad to," Lee said. Did this mean she had the job?

Lee followed Johanna downstairs to the machine area. Tiny Eve was kneeling beside an athletic-looking hunk lying on one of the futon frames with his knees bent and his feet glued to the upright bar.

"Relax the hip joint and breathe," Eve said to him. "You're clenching." She placed her hand in the crevice where his thigh met his hip. "This should be soft, Tom. Breathe into it."

Johanna held the door open spilling hot sunshine into the room.

"So," she said. "Tell me everything you know about Pilates."

"Um," Lee said, well..."

She followed her out the door into the warming afternoon. It was nearly three o'clock, which meant there was a good chance they'd be doused with a summer rain shower. Lee was totally unprepared for both the coming rain and her question about Pilates.

2

PILATES INSTITUTE

"When I am dead they will say, 'Pilates was right!' I am 50 years ahead of my time."
—**Joseph Pilates,** *New York* **magazine, 1964**

Focused on giving Lee 75 years of Pilates history, Johanna was unaware that she was struggling to keep up with her as they walked, briskly, down Palace Avenue. Without breaking pace or a sweat, Johanna oohed over a newborn in its carriage, admired a classic mustang's leather interior, did some window shopping, bemoaned the appearance of obese tourists in tasteless t-shirts, and explained the genesis of the Institute. Lee, hot, winded, and embarrassed by the clanking of her jewelry, imagined herself in *Glamour* magazine on the fashion don'ts page with a black bar shielding her true identity.

"The thing is..." Johanna said, "In the mid-sixties there were only three Pilates studios in the world, all in Manhattan." Johanna's stride was long and confident, her arms in rhythm with her legs. Unlike Eve or Margaret, whose actions seemed dance precise and choreographed,

Johanna's movements were fast, spontaneous, almost unpredictable. Lee, wearing flat, comfortable sandals, kept rushing to stay abreast.

Weaving past slower strollers, Johanna continued. "Back then, no one 'worked out' and people didn't obsess about eating. But I'd read a fascinating article about Joe in *Harper's Bazaar* and was intrigued. He believed physical fitness was the first requisite for happiness. You know what he said once? 'There is no hope for world peace if the members of the United Nations cannot do my first five mat exercises.' I'm known for making dramatic pronouncements which is probably why I was attracted to his persona." She laughed out loud while digging her sunglasses out of her shoulder bag.

A teenage boy in a Dr. Dre t-shirt and huge baggy jeans walked toward them carrying his skateboard. " Yo," he said.

Johanna glanced over the rim of her sunglasses. "Sam, hello. Nice shirt."

As they raced past she mused about rappers. "Sam is my older son's friend. They're both into rap. When my boys were younger, I dragged them to Bernstein rehearsals at Tanglewood, Lincoln Center, jazz concerts, *Cats*, and *Chorus Line*——you name it. Now they want this. So why do you think that white, privileged kids love rap?"

It wasn't a rhetorical question. She wanted Lee's opinion. Without an answer or breath to propel a response, Lee managed to shrug and raise her eyebrows while keeping in step. Johanna kept going, literally.

"Maybe it's the names. Dr. Dre, Pubic Enemy, Aceyalone, Tupac Shakur. They are intriguing. That's the problem with the name Pilates. It's not intriguing, but, trust me, there's plenty of intrigue."

"It is hard to pronounce," offered Lee.

"And to understand. Yolanda, my housekeeper, wonders why I've started a religious organization. My neighbor, who teaches Classics at St. John's College, says our name sounds like a Greek culture institute. And worse, its trademarked and owned by someone in New York."

Lee's mind drifted to the breakfast burrito in her fridge. Normally she ate the whole thing, but today with the interview and all she had been a bit rushed. Now she was starving.

"So where was I?.." Johanna forged on, "I tried Pilates, 1966, and loved it. Then, in 1970, the fitness boom starts and I went aerobic like everyone else. 'Go for the burn. No pain no gain.' I thought it was boring, plus it didn't feel right.

"When I ran in Riverside Park, I felt as if my face was falling, my vagina was dropping, and that my knees were giving out. I quit all that and went back to Pilates. I am so grateful that I saw the light before I really messed up my body."

Lee had never heard anybody mention her vagina during a job interview before, but Johanna didn't pause, just continued talking until they arrived at Santa Fe Subscription, a café and magazine store. Lee went there often to surreptitiously page through *Art Forum* so she could keep up with the literature without paying for it.

The door jingled as Lee pushed it open. "So. . ." Johanna said, as they both entered. Right away, Lee picked up the sharp coffee aroma and the even sharper stares of their fellow customers as Johanna speed walked to the long magazine racks at the back.

"Late eighties," Johanna recounted. "We leave New York and move here. There's no Pilates, of course, but I'm playing tennis, skiing, doing the matwork." She bent down beneath the travel magazine section to the floor and grabbed a *New York Times*. "But then, after a while, I get a pain in my neck that no massage could relieve. Everyone said it was the stress. There are fabulous body workers here, but, no surprise, I went to see an osteopath, they're doctors you know."

Suddenly, Johanna spun around and sped off to the Diet and

Fitness section, announcing to no one in particular that she had to check out the latest diet.

"What are you looking for?" Lee inquired.

"*Women's Fitness*," she said. "Well, Meredith said there's an article about aerobics losing steam. I've been expecting this trend to cool. Here it is in print."

She looked up from the magazine and began reading out loud the headlines: *"The Top Five Fat Burning Exercises, Summer Recipes that Really Burn Fat, Cross Train to Burn Fat Faster, Lose 5 Pounds in a Weekend with the Revolutionary Fat Burning Diet, Secrets of Celebrity Fat Burners."*

"No wonder it's been so hot here this summer. Maybe all this fat burning is causing the ozone depletion," Johanna commented with a delighted laugh, before resuming her Institute chronology.

"So the osteopath says to me: 'Johanna, C4 is locked. I think you should visit this woman in town who does some kind of movement therapy on unusual equipment'."

"So I go to see her, and that's how I met Eve Gentry! Can you believe it? Her Pilates studio was just a five-minute walk from my house! I'd been in Santa Fe for three years, and there she was, virtually in my back yard!"

Abruptly, she stopped speaking and looked at Lee.

"Wow," Lee said, hoping to pitch her enthusiasm at a level acceptable to Johanna. "That's incredible."

"Yes, it is amazing. Is there any magazine you'd like while we are here?"

There were a few publications Lee strongly desired, but decided now was not the time for gifts before she was even hired.

Johanna, still moving and speaking: "God I love the smell in here. Not just the coffee, which is actually very good, but also the newsprint. The aroma of information: so much to savor, so much to think about. Don't you love that?

"Okay, where was I? Oh. Yes. Eve. Anyway, discovering Eve reminded me of how truly exceptional Pilates was and that someone should take it public.

"Then, one day, April 14th, 1991 to be exact, I'm reading the Times and there's this article about exercise. About how we're all sick and tired of being aerobics bunnies and Schwarzanenegger wannabes and that its time to go back to the real thing—Pilates! Just a mention, but you know timing is everything."

She took out her wallet, ready to pay the cashier.

"You know," she said, "The Pilates cult really didn't want the secret out. Clients didn't spread the word because they were protective of their Reformer time-slots. Teachers feared other teachers, afraid of competition. This was one very private club."

Putting back her change, they stepped outside where the afternoon sky foretold rain showers at any minute. She picked up her pace walking even faster despite the uneven sidewalks and her three-inch heels.

"Oh by the way," she said, without pausing. "The day I read that article was April fourteenth, my forty-fifth birthday. Now I'm not superstitious or anything, but still I can't help thinking that was a sign."

"Forty-fifth?" Lee said, a bit taken back "Forty-fifth?"

"How old did you think I was?"

"Well, I was figuring, uh, mid-thirties."

Johanna smiled at the compliment while nakedly scrutinizing Lee's skin. "Thanks. Yes, Pilates is anti-aging for the body, but you also have to do something to protect your skin at 7000 feet up. Here's my secret, always wear lots of foundation and use Evian Brumisateur. Always."

The sky crackled with the warnings of thunder so Johanna moved even faster.

"So where was I?" she asked herself. "Oh yes. Birthday, article. Yes. So the very next day, I convinced Eve and Margaret to start the Institute. In six weeks, we'd drawn up a partnership agreement, incorporated, rented a space, moved Eve's studio and set up the Institute."

The sky turned greenish grey and the air chilled as crackling thunder grew more insistent.

"We're not going to make it." She notched up another gear so they were practically running. "So," she said, "ask me some questions."

Lee could barely breathe. She dropped back; worrying that Johanna wouldn't hire her if she saw her panting.

She took a huge breath and called ahead: "So Pilates is a type of exercise, then?"

Johanna favored her with a collegial laugh as they neared the building. "Yesssss. What did you think it was?"

Lee tried to control her gasping, to no avail. "I don't

know," she exhaled. "Those machines and everything...."

"You mean the apparatus?" Johanna prompted. "That reminds me, let's talk about the Encyclopedia. What typefaces do you like?"

As the rain started to soak their clothes, Johanna arrived at the door and held it open for Lee who followed close behind. Inside and drenched, she pulled the newspaper and magazine from the paper bag. "We need to copy this article on aerobics and use it. So, you didn't answer my question. Typographic style?"

"Does this mean I'm hired?" Lee asked.

"Of course you're hired," she said. "Don't tell me you can't start right away. What was your name again?"

"Lee."

"Great. The Encyclopedia should look classic yet modern, but no Helvetica. How do you feel about Garamond with Futura?"

"I feel 100 percent about Garamond," Lee said.

"Any other questions?" Johanna asked hurriedly.

Lee wondered if they had a microwave; she could not remember seeing anything upstairs except for the guy in the shorts and the skeleton. Giggling from a bit of lightheadedness, Lee realized she had gone from being hungry for work to being hungry at work.

"Not really," she replied.

"Good, lets get started." Johanna said while leading the way through the different pieces of 'apparatus.' On one of the machines, a tall, slender teenage girl was balancing on her tailbone on top of a box while pulling herself forward and back with her hands holding leather straps. Margaret watched over her, speaking gently, reassuringly.

"That's Bernadette," Johanna said as she went upstairs. "She's applied to the dance program at Julliard."

Johanna was halfway up the stairs when she called back. "Lee," she said. "We need a database too. Did Margaret tell you about the database?"

Lee glanced at Margaret who looked up from her client and held two fingers up. She mouthed the words, 'two speeds.'

Up above, Lee heard the tell-tale ping of the Macintosh turning on, an enormous thunderclap, then a disconcerting pop.

When Lee got to the top of the stairs, Johanna was standing in the dim office shaking her head at the darkened Macintosh. "Another power outage," she said. "As if we have time for this now."

Lee surmised that Johanna's deadlines were largely self-imposed, but knew the delay from the power outage truly frustrated her. Inaction wasn't in her play book.

Johanna put the magazines on the all-purpose Mission table and passed Lee a legal pad. "You're going to become an expert on Pilates, so write this down," she said.

3

PUBLICITY

"The Pilates body? Long slender thighs and calves, a flat tummy, a strong back, and a high tushie."
—*Elle* Magazine, 1991

When Lee began at the Pilates Institute, plans for its inaugural training workshop were well underway. Johanna was poised like a champion surfer waiting to ride the crest of a major wave into shore. An *Elle* magazine article, published the month the workshop took place, was her wave, and the Institute she'd only recently visualized and made real was the vehicle she'd mount to guide Pilates on to the mainland and to mainstream success.

Elle's four-page tribute to the Pilates Method titled *"The Early Morning Secret of Dancers"* named Katharine Hepburn, Gregory Peck, Martha Graham, Baryshnikov, Sigourney Weaver, Jasmine Guy, Kristi Yamaguchi and other fans as being in on the secret. *"Those in the know benefit because the Pilates apparatus and exercises were designed so that you just couldn't cheat,"* said *Elle.*

Talk about timing, even Margaret dropped her usual reserve and commented, "We're an overnight sensation after only 70 years of obscurity."

"Let's change that to hard work. An overnight sensation after 70 years of hard work," Johanna added. The *Elle* article confirmed that her instincts were correct and that the Institute was onto something big, that Pilates was ready to go public.

Johanna knew that Pilates' previous failure to catch on was not just because it was sophisticated exercise, the reason its adherents claimed. The dearth of clients was because no American since 1970 was interested in any exercise that was not 'fat burning'. Thus, training to become a Pilates teacher and investing your life savings from your dance career earnings to outfit a Pilates studio was just pointless. No clients, no professional organization, no teacher training programs, no teachers, no studios was the result.

Before she, Margaret and Eve moved into their new quarters, Johanna launched her new industry. The Institute's first mission was creating a qualified cadre of Pilates instructors. For the Institute to succeed, for its initial workshop to be well attended, she had to first identify anybody and everybody with professional ties to Pilates. Kent Hemel, who fabricated most of the Pilates' apparatus—Reformers and Cadillacs—provided his list, 225 names, although only a hundred were still in the game. When thirty percent of those contacted signed up for the workshop, Johanna saw immediately the pent-up demand. When she published the Pilates Forum, their newsletter, they heard from teachers neither they nor Hemel knew existed. The industry was beginning to take shape and now they had to make sure that everyone knew that this was happening in Santa Fe, and not in New York.

Johanna, working all the angles, knew that Lee was keyed into the happenings in Santa Fe and asked her to create an insiders guide for the workshop attendees. If they loved Santa Fe as much as they did Pilates, they'd return for sure. Lee, who'd been absorbing massive amounts of information about Pilates, noted again Johanna's 'cover all the bases' style. This was Lee's first real creative opportunity to contribute to the work of the Institute. Being a part of this tiny Pilates cult that 'according to the book of Johanna' was going to reshape America, was starting to feel like her mission, too.

Using a one to five chilies rating system, Lee picked out her favorite places. Her five chilies destinations included: Ten Thousand Waves, the Folk Art Museum, the Palace of the Governors, Morningstar Gallery, Shidoni, and Bandelier. In between finishing the workshop materials, she answered a gazillion questions from early workshop attendees who were ready with the typical tourist questions: red and green chilies served together is called "Christmas style," try echeverria for altitude headaches, and yes, ristras can be shipped.

She was at the center of the action and hoped Margaret would notice her enthusiasm and expertise to the extent she was certain Johanna already had. That afternoon, Lee, who had never found a microwave among the many apparatus and gizmos in the Institute, darted out for a quick coffee and brownie to keep her nerves in check. Johanna spotted her at the doorway.

"Lee, great idea to copy the stories about Joe that Eve saved all these years. These young Pilates teachers haven't read them. Christ, they weren't born yet. *Sports Illustrated* in '62, The *New York Times* in '63, *New York Herald Tribune* in '65.

"Joe got plenty of press, but Americans weren't ready to move a muscle. A friend 's parents, they came here from Austria after the war, loved to tell the story of their evening walks. Invariably, a neighbor driving by would stop and offer them a ride. When they explained that they were taking exercise, the reaction was total bewilderment.

"When Joe arrived here in 1920 from Germany, he found a physical fitness wasteland. Today we spell it w-a-i-s-t-land and it's huge. He was so far ahead. If he were alive today to see body conditioning morph from non-existent to big business, with fat burning as its *raison d'etre*, he would die all over again."

Lee, who still hadn't figured out why Pilates people thought that exercise and fat burning were non sequitors, had poured over Eve's clippings going back six decades so she could get up to speed.

"I just don't get it. Why did his Method die out? Is it because he died?" Lee asked Johanna.

"It didn't die out! It never got going! Everybody was thin then," Johanna erupted. Lee knew a diatribe was coming which was her chance to learn stuff she hadn't even thought about before.

"Athletes and dancers were the only exercisers. That's how Joe survived. Then one day in the forties, George Balanchine, followed by Martha Graham, found their way to his studio. For the next two decades, he rehabbed their dancers and a few *au courant* New Yorkers. Finally in 1964, Geraldine Stutz, the President of Bendel's, invited him to put a Pilates studio in her store, only the chicest retail emporium in the world. Three years later he died just as the fitness trend was starting. Between then and now the Pilates Method just sputtered along, losing its decades'-long lead."

But now this lost lead was about to be regained because of the *Elle* article, four pages of raves about the Pilates Method that had just been published in the October 1991 issue.

"We need to merchandise the *Elle* article," Johanna said as if it were a concha belt at Ortega's. "I'll call editors who might remember me from my other life in the beauty business. Make sure that they saw it. Lee can set up free lessons for them with Deborah Lavey in New York. She trained with Eve, which is a big plus since we happen to be only a mere 2000 miles away."

A week later Johanna reported on her follow-up call with Susan Cheeve at *Vogue* after Susan's lesson: "Susan says that she didn't sweat, she wasn't even sore the next day. That ridiculous "no pain/no gain" mantra undermines everything Joe stood for. We have to get other editors to test-drive Pilates while the *Elle* article is still hot and they're more likely to be convinced. Sooner than later we have to get around this resistance. They are hooked on pain and don't want to give it up."

"Are New Yorkers nuts? Relieved, that's what I would feel if someone told me I didn't have to kill myself several times a week," cracked Lee, "Not that this body is showing the effects of sweating on a treadmill and going for the burn in the weight room."

Johanna, listening to Lee's comment, heard it as a request for help and turned to Margaret. "Is she ready?"

"For what?" Lee asked.

"For your makeover," explained Margaret, more animated then ever before.

"So, if you are really ready, we can offer you only the best body and diet people in the world. And, one more thing: We get full rights to the before and after photos."

"Where's the camera? Take my body! You can even use that damn measuring tape," Lee bravely offered.

"We'll fix your body, inside and out. Margaret and Meredith will double team you," said Johanna, satisfied and pleased that she had made another Pilates convert.

4

MEREDITH LUCE RD, MS, LN

"The only good news dieters seem to hear these days comes from commercials and ads...notwithstanding, a national panel last week confirmed that more than 90 percent of dieters fail to keep the pounds off permanently. In fact, whether they have shed 15 pounds or 50, most regain nearly all they've lost within a year."
—The New York Times, 1992

Johanna was pacing again, up and down the length of the office. These staccato laps, however, were not borne of dismay or of pursuit of intellectual clarity. This was a happy dance. Her friend Meredith was about to lead Lee down the road to eternal eating wisdom. "Do you know how lucky you are? Forget for a moment all the letters after her name and summa cum laude, too. What I should really say is forget for a moment the size of your thighs and focus on the big picture. And, I don't mean the 10 pounds photography adds.

"You're lucky, because Meredith is going to teach you how to eat. This means you will save yourself thousands of hours worrying about whether you should follow the nutritional information the media reports on, then revises, but never apologizes for the correction which follows six months later: like margarine is better for you than butter.

Sorry, margarine is not good. Forget butter and margarine and use olive oil.

"Trust me, Ms. Lee Raney, you will be thanking me for the rest of your life. Which, post-Meredith, is guaranteed to be a long one, and obviously, a much lighter one."

Meredith Luce MS, RD LN was the nutritionist savvy health editors dialed when in need of a sound bite on the latest diet trend. A long time friend of Johanna's, Meredith had a private practice in New York for women who could not be too thin or too rich. Lee was about to join her too thin celebrity clientele. She prayed that the too rich part would follow after her makeover.

Lee phoned Meredith immediately after Eve's workshop ended to get started. Meredith began as always with the client history. "So when was the last time you saw 110 pounds? I always tell new clients that setting weight goals they haven't seen since junior high is a hard way to start. Although at least with you that was only 15 years ago. With many of my clients, Eisenhower was still in the White House!

"So Lee, let's talk about New Mexican cuisine."

"I love it. All of it. Burritos, tacos, quesadillas, enchiladas, don't hold the sour cream and guacamole. Yes, always.

Salt on my margaritas, gracias," Lee said, happily visualizing her favorites.

"Okay, I see the picture. First of all, when you eat at Tomasita's, let's say, or Tortilla Flats, you need to recognize that there is too much food on the plate. Believe me, it's in the vicinity of 30 percent too mucho," Meredith stated emphatically.

"But how do you know this?"

"I have eaten there. And their 'portions' are typical. Typical of most ethnic restaurants, really."

"Ethnic portions differ from American ones?" Lee grimaced, thinking about all the lost opportunities to get down to Mexico she had squandered these last seven years. Too late now.

"Basic American cooking was simple. Didn't we all grow up with a main dish, usually meat or fish, and two sides, a starch and a vegetable? With this combo we knew how much to eat. Then came dessert, which everyone knew was 'fattening'. Anyway, when Mexican, Japanese, Indian foods, you name it, started showing up in the seventies, we couldn't visualize correct portions. And since these foods are relatively cheap to begin with, ethnic restaurants load up the plates. They can charge more and everyone goes home happy with the perceived value of combo plates and baskets of fried whatnots. Grande is their motto."

"Whoa, I have to give up my favorite restaurants because I'm not sure how much to eat?" Lee moaned.

"Hold on, I don't recommend giving up what you like. Eating diet foods you hate only leads to late-night binges. Just slow down, chew every bite so you really taste the food, check-in with yourself throughout the meal to see when you're satiated, and then simply STOP. Now let's talk about snacking. It's simple. Don't," said Meredith sternly.

"Well that's not hard in this office. We don't even have a coffee machine," responded Lee.

"That's our Johanna," chuckled Meredith. "She rejects office coffee and calls it 'brown water' whenever it's politely offered. And then she doesn't understand why people are so put off with her. But, I think both you and I know that the people she puts off don't know her, don't get her. She believes that drinking brown water ruins your palate and that leads to fatness so she's helping them to stay thin.

"Has she told you her Bendel's story, the one about where she had the epiphany that 'saved' her from yo-yo dieting?"

"You can diet at Bendel's?" Lee marveled.

"Not really, the only thing you can lose at Bendel's is your bankroll. So, mid sixties, Bendel's. Johanna, brand new to Pilates, is on a Reformer and another woman—also named Johanna—is on the adjacent one. They're both in their twenties and the same size. Probably a four, since the Bendel's doorman stopped anyone larger from entering. Anyway, they both rise and stand in front of full-length mirrors in their itsy bitsy pastel leotards that reveal every curve. Our Johanna observes that the other Johanna simply has the better body—a quarter of an inch less across the hips, a more rounded chest, and so on—structural stuff you could see if you bothered to compare both under a microscope. In that singular moment, Johanna had her body epiphany. She 'understood' that beating up her body by dieting, starving, sweating was absolutely pointless. She was 'saved.'"

Meredith laughed retelling the story and told Lee to check in with her in a week. Before signing off, she included her toothbrush-dieting tip. "If you feel hungry, brush your teeth until the sensation passes. Can you think of any food that tastes good mixed with toothpaste?"

Lee already knew from a photo in the office what Meredith looked like: blond, classic features, perfect teeth and a size two. The photo was part of a big magazine article about her and her famous family. Her grandfather pioneered the modern news magazine and built his into a publishing colossus, America's most successful magazines.

Lee doubted that Meredith ever experienced the body issues her clients agonized over daily. Her friendly, low-key attention and counsel flattered Lee. Knowing that someone with Meredith's pedigree was interested in her made Lee feel giddy, as if she were part of Meredith's New York world. Soon, she too would be off to a Missoni show or a late lunch at Le Cirque. Meredith's life must be so glamorous.

Then Lee told herself to stop being a jerk. Sure, Meredith could afford to live the life of a social butterfly, but that wasn't how she spent her time. She didn't do the homework that earned her all those degrees sitting at a table at the '21 Club' or some other famous restaurant where a meal cost more than her monthly food allowance. She doubted that Meredith spent much of her non-existent free time marveling over her own wonderfulness. Like Johanna, she was an educator, almost a crusader.

Lee recalled a conversation between them just the week before. Johanna, pacing the office, listened to Meredith on the speaker phone vent her frustrations.

"Everyday I counsel women who struggle with their weight, suffer from eating disorders, and hate their bodies.

Then, I speak to the editors at *Self* or *Redbook* and hear more stories of desperation. Women are becoming afraid of food."

"Everyone only wants to know the next "miracle" food. When is the public going to realize there is no miracle, much less miracle food? Here we are in 1991 when one half of the population is over-weight. Weight Watches started in '64 and almost 30 years later we are even fatter. Let's go after these attitudes, Meredith, write something for our Pilates Forum. "

"You're such an optimist. You think that if we just offer logic and correct information, light will be shed and the problem resolved. Johanna, this growing—excuse the pun—trend is becoming ominously dark," worried Meredith.

"I think this can all be attributed to the public's desire to avoid personal responsibility," Johanna lectured. "Instead of eating smart and pushing away from the table before they've eaten double what they need, they want somebody else to take responsibility for their reckless behavior.

"If I said this to anyone but you, I'd be crucified, but I trace this craziness to the tobacco litigation. We've known for decades that smoking kills. Yet when plaintiff attorneys during the tobacco litigation cross examined witnesses with emphysema or lung cancer, who smoked two or three packs a day for 30 years, these people claimed they didn't know that cigarettes were bad for your body or addictive because the warnings weren't on pack labels when they first started to light up.

"Hello! These people can't walk up a flight of stairs, and they can't sleep through the night because they're too busy hacking and spitting up phlegm. Ugh. They get bronchitis and sinusitis and five other upper respiratory illnesses regularly, and even if they feel nothing or ignore their health, think about the physical signs! They can't see the yellow teeth, stained fingernails, and the ugly broken capillaries on their faces? And, then, there's the smell. They and their clothes reek!

"For Christ's sake, Meredith, vanity or health, take either or both. Nobody seemed to be shocked that these people hadn't a clue. Everyone went along with their sad stories of victimization, so that the only ones held responsible for the smokers' infirmities were the ones with the huge vaults of dough. Now we have no-fault everything. There's no personal responsibility anymore. Tell me this isn't what contributes to this food craziness."

"I don't know. Aren't you stretching it here a bit?" wavered Meredith.

"Maybe. But I'll bet you that in ten years someone is

going to sue McDonald's because they are fat. Like obese."

"I'm not betting, but I'll take you to Le Bernadin if you're proven right. Then we'll take the next flight to Paris."

"Deal. But in the meantime write something—anything for us. *Self* Magazine can't compete with this offer of total editorial freedom."

" You do know that your former dancers, now Pilates teachers, are all into 'good food/bad food'?"

"I know you're right. It's ironic too, because Joe was carnivorous and also smoked huge cigars and drank a pint of Scotch regularly."

"Remember, he's been dead for decades. Everyone was like that back then. Carbohydrates. Triglycerides. These words are harder to pronounce than Pilates. Nutrient chat was for food cultists, most of whom were also nudists. If Joe was still in his swim suit and terrorizing his students, even he might have traded the Scotch for H_2O and veggies."

"Or maybe he'd eat salmon every other Thursday when its raining in Bermuda," Johanna added with sarcasm.

"Or maybe they'd have him waiting 30 minutes after eating protein before ingesting fruit. Remember *Fit for Life?*"

"How do you deal with these crazy diet manipulations? I am giving you a forum. Tell these food obsessers that that they are nuts. Not the food, though. I love almonds."

"OK, I'll send you something next week. My client has just arrived. She's going to swear that she's followed the diet I gave her down to every last comma, and she still gained three pounds. Bye."

5

LEGAL LIMBO

"Bye-bye burn, hello balance. Welcome to fitness in the 21st century. For a sneak preview, let us take you to planet Pilates, a brave new workout world where muscles streamline ballerina-lean, where body meets mind and moving is mellow."
—Shape Magazine, 1992

In preparation for the first workshop, the Institute team focused on documenting Joe's exercises and philosophy. This would be the first time Joe's life work would be gathered into a coherent body. Descriptions of the movements, how to modify them, the cues that best help instructors help clients, what positions should be avoided, and appropriate spring resistances, would all be included. Every word needed to be precisely crafted.

An advisory board made up of those who, like Eve, had trained directly with Joe was formed and consulted on specifics. All of the board members but one, Roberta, were active, helpful, and responsive.

"Nothing back from Roberta," Johanna questioned as she entered the office and moved a cup of brown water off the cover of the upcoming Forum blueline.

"Not yet. Maybe we should call her again," Lee suggested.

"Let's not and say we did. My guess is she's upset that we are letting 'her' secrets out." Johanna's tone was heavy with sarcasm.

Margaret shot a knowing glance at Lee.

Lee knew that Roberta had a connection to the ownership of the Pilates label, this hard to pronounce name. She had heard that Roberta fancied herself a royal lady-in-waiting and the anointed Pilates heiress. And although she didn't legally own the trademark, she believed that she was the only one who taught the real Pilates. But, Lee just couldn't wrap her mind around the implications of this bizarre situation. Her friends still drew a blank when she mentioned where she worked or what she was doing.

Although Lee saw a drama brewing, she secretly relished the thought of the catfight ahead. She knew Johanna had consulted two lawyers whose carefully worded opinions on trademark issues sounded more like double talk than legal advice. Realizing that these two were lightweights in the intellectual property department, Johanna found another attorney, an actual trademark expert, whose opinion was succinct: retain him to file a Cancellation of Trademark in the U.S. Patent and Trademark Office in Washington DC.

"Is the trademark valid or not?" Lee asked one morning after Johanna had hung up from another expensive conversation with their latest legal maven.

"It's complicated because neither Joe nor his wife Clara registered their name. In some countries, like the UK, only the person with the name can register it. Joe died in 1967, Clara in 1977, and then Roberta waited a respectful time—five years, I think—and registered it."

"Doesn't Roberta say that Pilates was a gift from Clara?"

"All we know is Clara hired her to run the studio after Joe died. But the word on the street was that Roberta was not short listed for the job. No one else wanted it."

"She doesn't have what we call a 'head for business'."

"A friend of mine, a client at the studio until it closed in 1988, said that their annual sales were $20,000. Annual. The entire year."

"With that resume she's not going to get hired in this lifetime. "

"I don't think she's looking for her next job. She's just waiting for her next Prince. She's been engaged twice before, but neither one made her the Pilates queen. But this new guy, Steve Gross, who is a Physical Therapist and knows Pilates, is making eyes at her now. This could be the one."

"Maybe they will fall in love and just sail off together into the sunset."

"Dream on. He's not only a PT. He's a clever businessman, very connected, and an excellent therapist. Plus his sister is a lawyer. This is a combination we don't need."

"Why does this Steve guy need Roberta?"

"Well, not for her training insights. He really knows Pilates and the body, but he'll probably have to go along with her explanations of how 'Uncle Joe' did it. He can't claim ownership of the trademark without his beloved Roberta because to make the legal case continuity has to be proved. And, that's where she fits in.

"This will be embarrassing for him professionally, but then money is such a good balm."

"What's his next move? Picking out the ring?"

"No he's got a long way before that. First he has to find the guy who bought the TM from Roberta and her partners in the mid-eighties. This guy has been in hiding since 1988 when the Feds closed the Pilates studio. Then he has to convince this guy to sell him the trademark. If he gets it, then he proposes to the lovely Roberta. If she says yes—and she will—they get hitched, but there is no time for a honeymoon. He, no his lawyers, will have to contact all the people who use the name and get them to stop. Wait. I forgot one tiny detail. His lawyers have to find these offensive Pilates people first."

"Piece of cake."

"It seems like a long shot, but it could happen. Legal actions. Cease and desist letters. Trademark infringement lawsuit. We'd be first. He'll need a public hanging."

"But Eve is part of the Institute and we know she has been using the P word since 1968. I thought Clara helped her set up her studio, even had a Reformer made for her."

"Exactly what our lawyer will say, but the thing is so fuzzy. And the law is on the side of the trademark holder, possession is nine tenths of the law. After all, they paid Uncle Sam—not Uncle Joe—for the trademark."

Lee pondered all this. "Do you think it's too late to change the name of the Institute? You said his name connects our members. And Joe deserves the credit—he is probably hanging from the Cadillac watching us right now."

"Right, and if he hadn't expected to live forever, he might have settled on how his name and his method would be preserved. Instead he was working on how he would be preserved."

"Do you think that he understood this trade-mark stuff?"

"Doubtful. Very few people do. From what I know about this subject, convoluted as it is, this mark can't stand up. We're going to file for Cancellation so we'll know soon, I hope."

The more Lee learned about the TM subject, the more she realized that a catfight would be only a skirmish in a long battle beginning with the Cancellation Action. Maybe this was why Johanna resorted to humor to keep her sanity. The Pilates name, fat burning, and miracle foods provided so much fodder for comedy.

"Is the pilot in?" deadpanned Johanna as she clunked the receiver down onto the table. "These calls are all over the place. If we intimidate or embarrass them though they won't want to hear about Pilates. The calls are really starting to trickle in—they've heard Pilates is exercise, it's a machine, it's a method, it's a man. Yesterday, someone was at the door wanting answers. Even when they get the Pilates part, they still don't understand what we are trying to do. It seems as if Americans only understand retail. Doesn't anyone work for companies that create, not just sell, things?"

When they had run out of riffs on the P word, Johanna would joke with Lee about the latest fat burning methods. Johanna was certain the public would buy a book about unusual calorie burning methods that could also showcase Lee's artistic talents: "What do you think ? Does 'passing the buck' burn more calories than 'dragging one's heels'? For me this one is obvious. Passing is so much easier. It's only worth 25 calories. While dragging is definitely over 100. You don't even have to be smart to figure this out."

Whenever legal discussions got too tense, Johanna would add to the list of calorie burning methods which, of course, never included exercise. Like 'swallowing your pride', 'beating around the bush', and 'pushing your luck'. Sometimes she referenced Pilates as in 'Threatening People with an Invalid Trademark'. It was all a game to distract Johanna from the real threats and Lee gladly played along.

"If we assign too many calories burned to let's say 'Climbing the ladder of success,' corporations would be stampeded," Lee suggested.

"That's the beauty of our system. We can discourage

behaviors we don't like by keeping the calories artificially low."

"But what if people don't accept our counts?"

"I've never seen a calorie. Have you? The entire country has been counting them for 35 years and no one has ever seen one. It's just a numbers game. It proves my favorite line, 'Figures don't lie, but liars do figure.'"

When they had exhausted calorie burning, Johanna always could riff on a topic dear to the hearts of millions— water. This subject alone proved to Johanna that Americans were nuts when it came to their bodies.

"I know water can be holy. That cleanliness is next to godliness. But where does it say that it has to be bottled?" Johanna would ask out loud.

Lee couldn't stop herself from explaining. "People feel it is healthier. Can't you see those photos of mountain springs?"

"It's a marketing miracle. Safe, free, available and tastes good from the tap and Americans are spending billions to buy it in bottles. A Pilates trainer told me that tea, or juice, or soda don't count toward her daily infusion of eight 8-ounce glasses of water. Duh. They're all 98 percent water. This isn't just gullibility. It is so mixed up with detoxing and cleansing and being good and eating healthy that I wanted to grab that huge bottle that is permanently attached to the end of her arm. I would probably have to amputate her arm just to get her to drop it. It's so stupid. Do you know that the 8 x 8 directive left out a vital fact?"

"No way."

"The landmark 1945 article about water left out that the almighty 64 ounce commandment was contained in a balanced diet. Almost everything we eat has water. I mean our bodies are 80 percent water."

Lee grimaced: "No wonder I feel bloated all the time."

"That's probably why W. C. Fields never drank water."

"Ugh...but he did like liquid refreshment I understand."

"Supposedly he drank two double martinis every day before breakfast, but I think that is a bit of an exaggeration."

"And on the subject of H_2O?"

"A reporter asked him if he also drank water and he reportedly replied, "Hell, no. Fish piss in water.""

"You can't rest your case on that line, particularly in Santa Fe."

"Maybe not. But Lee, do you get what I have been saying here over and over? All these health admonitions are so oversimplified."

Lee was vaguely aware that maybe, perhaps, Johanna was onto something. Maybe this and 20 other things were connected, but right now she just needed a coffee with sugar and cream and a smallish brownie. At least she wasn't detoxing.

6

THE FUNDAMENTALS WORKSHOP

*"The Pilates Method, an old practice (that) works
well for a New Age, the technique includes resistance
training and stretching to promote flexibility, toning,
and mental and physical harmony."*
—Minneapolis Star Tribune, 1993

Monday morning after Eve's workshop, Lee was
exhausted, cramped. Fortunately today's job description
called for sitting and reviewing the video tapes, her video
tapes, her first film opus. Right before the curtain went up
so to speak, Johanna told her to video Eve's workshop. After
a five minute tutorial that taught her too little about how
to work the equipment, she sensed that great style might
have to carry the day if she were to succeed in her anointed role as the 'official Pilates videographer'.

During the intense weekend, Johanna played John
Huston while Lee moved the camera freely about, trying
not to trip anyone with the cords.

"Once we are famous I'll get you a key grip, but for
now keep it together. And try looking at me. How else will
you notice my cues of when to shoot?" said Johanna.

For two days they had shadowed Eve, trying many angles, in order to capture the tiniest, nuanced movements as she deconstructed advanced Pilates exercises. Not always in agreement, Lee begrudgingly waited for Johanna's signal to shoot. Now this quiet morning, Lee was relishing being alone with the tapes, free to edit and prepare for the 'post mortem' at Johanna's home two days later.

Wednesday evening all players gathered at Johanna's eastside estate, a first for Lee. She had wisely eaten ahead, unsure whether food was a part of Johanna's lifestyle.

As with all homes on the historic eastside—everything from the location of the house, its front door, and where to park, was unclear. This was strangely purposeful, as if this mystery added to the casual, really understated look. Give me a break, Lee thought. Whereas in Boston it was quite clear what was and wasn't an alley, here narrow dirt roads were de rigueur. The more sought-after the property, the narrower the road. So this was what that bantered about phrase 'behind adobe walls' was all about. Once inside the walls, tiny solar spotlights lit the walkway to a gate which led to a courtyard which connected to the actual front door. Lee guessed the requisite *vigas, bancos, kivas, nichos,* Spanish doors, Sautillo tile floors and hand plastered walls would all be present and accounted for. But she expected a few surprises. For sure, Johanna would have a signature style. She was not disappointed.

Inside a ten-foot curving low couch anchored a sunken living room with ceilings that seemed as high as the altitude. Through huge windows looking past Camino del Monte Sol, the Sangre Mountains rose in the distance. Eve sat squarely in the middle of the couch viewing a large TV broadcast of a larger than life version of herself. Margaret sat next to her seemingly transfixed by the images. Johanna, carrying a silver tray of petit pain, duck paté and a dish of almond stuffed olives, joined them. A plate of thinly sliced pears sat on the kidney-shaped glass coffee table. Lee realized that there would be no house tour. Obviously, Johanna would consider it too nouveau riche.

"You can thank me now! Was this last minute videoing of Eve's workshop a stroke of brilliance. Now we can slowly replay it and analyze the reactions of these Pilates teachers," Johanna announced to the three of them.

On screen, Eve was demonstrating not only perfect form, but also offering instructive cues on alignment and the feel of the movement.

"You make Teaser look easy, Eve," observed Margaret.

"Like butter," giggled Lee, feeling a sense of comaraderie.

"In all my decades doing Pilates, Eve, all I ever

heard was 'use your powerhouse' while getting poked until I got it. Of course there was that other great correction: 'Make it look expensive'," said Johanna.

"We all learned Pilates that way. My teaching evolved because of need. There wasn't a Physical Therapist in this town when I moved here. Physicians recommended injured patients to me, but I couldn't teach them classical Pilates. But using my Bartenieff training, then Feldenkreis, I adapted Pilates so these patients could do it," explained Eve.

Lee interrupted, "Where is the Perrier, Johanna?"

"Lee, there's plenty of Perrier and Pellegrino. And, in the ice bucket on the bar, you will find perfect cubes of frozen Evian water which I made specially so that when they melt, they won't contaminate your pure mountain-fed spring water," Johanna teased.

"Thanks for going to all that trouble, but I'm switching to vodka. You can't get any purer than that," Lee retorted.

Johanna turned back to the video. "Everyone watch Eve. She's amazing."

Back on the screen, Lee's video had captured the almost surreal fluidity of Eve's movements and her voice as she talked her way through the moves. "We inhale, then imprint the spine. Now, initiating from deep in the abdominals, we float up into the V." Flowing like a chain of silver links, Eve peeled herself off the floor vertebra by vertebra. "And now we reverse the motion, slowly, one vertebra at a time, imprinting the spine back onto the floor," she said.

They watched the precision, the breathing, the alignment of the neck and head, the softness of the hip flexors, the hollowness of the belly. Nothing gripped. Nothing strained. Eve at eighty-one was able to perform these advanced moves perfectly, over and over again, while explaining the hows and the whys to the young workshop attendees, none of whom could approach her form. It was both intimidating and inspiring.

"Eve," Johanna said, leaning back into her dense sofa. "You are living proof that a spine doesn't have to age."

Eve shrugged. "Not bad for a woman who's had a stroke."

"Truly?" asked Lee.

"Truly, I believe so." Eve felt that she'd suffered a stroke at some point in the last year, but her doctor was unconvinced. Her complaints seemed ridiculous when she could move with the grace of a cat. Like most dancers, she could isolate each vertebra and feel every cell. Johanna called them all 'body junkies,' half in jest, but she meant it as a compliment. Paying attention, body awareness, she deemed good, but body obsessions made her go nuts. "How do women lose it when it comes to their own bodies and fall for weird diet and exercise manipulations," she'd rail.

"If this weren't on the tape I wouldn't believe it," Johanna said suddenly "and I'm not a Pilates teacher."

"What is it?" Margaret asked.

Johanna pointed at the screen. "Look at these Pilates teachers. Eve's mini-moves, the exercises that teach how to feel the correct placement, are totally, totally new to them. Why don't they know this?"

Johanna rose from the sofa and started pacing which made her mind work even faster.

"These moves are the key to Pilates' accessibility and the credibility of our organization. Let's face it. The reasons why Pilates has never taken off are becoming obvious and they're not just name mumbo-jumbo. This is sophisticated exercise, but if it had been taught properly, it would already have an audience. It wouldn't be just a cult. What I am getting at is that our current crop of teachers didn't learn the bio-mechanics behind Joe's exercises. They are great movers. They have smart bodies. But do they know how to break down complex exercises like Teaser or Short Spine for the regular folks? Like the billions of bodies that aren't naturally coordinated or balanced? These teachers learned only the Pilates exercises from Roberta , Karola, and Rob and other first generation teachers. But to learn how to teach them to humans who are not dancers, who don't move well, required too many years of apprenticeship, of observing and trying to figure it out."

Lee didn't know much about Roberta and Karola, two first generation teachers, but she'd heard a story about Rob Flacher that she thought made the secrecy point. Flacher, a former Martha Graham dancer and student of Joe's, opened his studio in Beverly Hills in 1971. With an *unlisted* phone number! Soon all the stars and starlets just had to have that number. Had to have their bodies gracing a Reformer. Talk about exclusivity. The harder it was to get a lesson—you know the drill. Well that's over. Johanna predicted the *Elle* magazine was going to blast open this secret cult. Thousands will be peering into the Yellow Pages. Right below pilots, pilot clubs, private pilots. But they're not going to find anything and not because the number is unlisted. There were only a handful of studios and most were cautious about using the P word anyway. Now the *Elle* article would change that and everything else, including her job.

Johanna returned to the sofa, grabbed the remote

control and fast-forwarded the image. "Look," she said. "Here's Eve teaching Rib Cage Arms and Imprinting to Susan Balack from Boulder. Then we see Susan doing Hundreds, our signature exercise. Susan's form has improved because she gets it first into her mind. Joe's favorite quote, 'It's the mind that moves the body.' Right? Eve's mini moves are the pre-Pilates exercises that will make teaching Joe's exercises so much better and easier."

"But Johanna, teachers are overwhelmed, there are so many exercises and spring settings and the sequences." Margaret said as she looked at Eve and Lee for verification. But Lee didn't want to respond. From her in-depth experience of one whole month, the exercise photo-montages of Joe on the Reformer and Joe on the Mat looked pretty similar. Ditto for the Cadillac. Plus they all looked just like the yoga stuff her friends were always trying to get her to do.

Johanna stood up and resumed pacing. "Look," she said. Pilates teachers have made the process of learning to teach tortuous. Starting with a knowledge of biomechanics and anatomy would have leveled the playing field because structurally we are all alike. Isn't that true? Other than the aliens, that is. Excuse me, I forgot. We are in New Mexico. They've already landed."

Lee, ignoring Johanna's New Mexican putdown, continued. "Since the *Elle* story, calls are pouring, not trickling in. People are asking where to find pilot classes in Dayton, Ohio. What should I tell them?"

Margaret and Eve laughed good-naturedly.

But Johanna didn't join in. Riffing on the pronunciation wasn't on her mind anymore. She was worried about the impact of the *Elle* article, and Lee couldn't understand why.

"The *Elle* article is fabulous!"

"Lee, Americans are not patient. They're now bored with aerobics and on to the next best thing. We're it, but we have to be accessible. Maybe there are 100 studios, but we need five times that number right now. And these few studios aren't where we need them. Look at Boulder, a hotbed of Pilates. Six studios in one small town. If you lined up all the Reformers there and placed them end to end, you could walk to Denver without ever touching the ground. Meanwhile there is probably not one Reformer in Arizona or Ohio or Nevada or most states," she raved.

Johanna's raving made Lee remember a card that Meredith had sent Johanna for her last birthday. It read, "Happy Birthday. You are a raving beauty." And inside— "Sometimes you are a beauty and sometimes you are just raving." Johanna loved it. Now she was raving. She wanted to get Pilates known, but she hadn't bargained for an impossible time schedule.

Johanna went on, "Yes Pilates is complex, but the current teacher training model is like typing using a hunt and peck system. Obviously, touch typing makes the process much more accurate and faster. This is just an analogy, but it explains a lot. Right now prospective teachers who aren't near a studio—the majority— have to relocate for a year just to do the exercises and then spend years apprenticing trying to understand them. This won't get us anywhere fast."

Eve and Margaret sat listening and taking it all in.

"And if we can train the trainers, set up certifying teacher training centers, you are talking about putting it all out. No secret handshakes," Eve said finally.

"Absolutely," Johanna responded. "No more secrets. We publish all the information. Prospective teachers will see the entire picture in the beginning. Not just the trees, but also the forest. Now they learn by osmosis, which is hardly efficient. We won't topple all the old ways, though. Joe's original students, let's call them the first generation, will be special. They can move up to Master Teacher. That's your title Eve."

"What about Roberta? She's on our Board of Advisors,"

"Her too," said Johanna. "I doubt she knows any anatomy or biomechanics. Maybe leaving out this vital information is her way of thwarting any competition."

Lee looked at Margaret who was more than intrigued.

"What about this idea? We re-shoot this workshop material and add Joe's classical matwork. We can produce a dynamic instructional video showing how Eve's mini moves, let's call them the Fundamentals, help one learn, not just the advanced exercises such as Teaser and Twist, but also the basics such as Roll Up and Single Leg Stretch. Won't this video help prospective teachers learn faster? And it will be a first. The very first Pilates video and we will own it," explained Margaret.

Johanna looked at Margaret and smiled, "And who says Pilates teachers don't know anything about business?"

7

THE PILATES VIDEO SHOOT

"Pilates is a marvelous method for developing the weakest of areas."
—New York magazine, 1991

"No, Priscilla. Don't grip. You need to hollow your abdomen. CUT!"

Priscilla and Sara, two former dancers, lying on their backs under the hot lights in the San Clemente Sound Studio, collapsed from frustration and exhaustion. They had been trying for an hour to perform one Pilates mat exercise that would satisfy Margaret. Rick, the cameraman, hit pause and the boom operator dropped her vertical arms and stood the big fuzzy microphone atop its boom pole at her side. In a director's chair next to Lee, Eve shook her head while smiling generously.

"They're trying," she whispered. "But they've never worked in a neutral pelvis. They don't know how to imprint the spine."

Margaret, who until now had been directing Priscilla through her hidden ear piece, rose from her chair, lay down next to Priscilla, and placed a hand under the small of her back. "You need to keep some air here. You're forcing it. Now...Raise your head slightly and lengthen. Nothing more."

Priscilla folded her long arms and legs into herself and rolled like a ball. "I thought I was doing that." Even as she rolled back and forth as a child moments before a tantrum, Priscilla was elegant in her muted pink leotard and white tights.

Margaret sat up and touched Priscilla's shoulder reassuringly. "I know, but you're tucking your pelvis and squeezing your butt. We want neutral."

On the adjacent mat Sara sat up, brushed her long red hair off her face, placed her elbows on her knees, and eyeballed her bag of trail mix on the floor by the sound recording utility cart. Lee remembered Meredith saying that grazing was an unfortunate occupational hazard that dancers couldn't avoid.

Margaret stood up and glided back to her director's chair. "Now let's do this again," she said. "You've almost integrated these concepts."

Sara and Priscilla shared a look then lay back down on

their blue mats, knees bent.

"Breathe into your back," Margaret said into her microphone. "And hollow your abdominals. Roll sound."

Nikki, the boom operator, raised her arms and the cameraman pressed his eye to the lens one more time. Margaret was clearly enjoying her command. Directing suited her. Although she had never produced a Pilates video, an exercise video—actually any video—and had watched very few, Margaret was able to juggle the dozens of necesary details without breaking a sweat. The Pilates concepts were in her bones. From her dancing career came a natural ease around wardrobe, makeup, set design, sound, lighting, props and rehearsals. What Margaret's dance experience didn't cover, Lee was there to assist with: catering, interviews, editing, contracts, and permits. Together they compressed six months work into 30 days. Not that Lee had any idea how long it should take to do anything now that she had acclimated to 'Johanna time'.

After four hours of Cervical Nods, Pelvic Bowls, Teasers and Single Leg Stretches, only three minutes of actual run time was 'in the can'. Meanwhile, Margaret's friend, Richard, was composing the background music. A title sequence and introduction featuring a Santa Fe travelogue were also in the works. Santa Fe's artistic community had bartered their services for Pilates lessons. Sara and

Priscilla had bartered their bodies to be part of the Institute's first certification program.

Sitting between Eve and Margaret, one eye on the clock and the other on the budget, Lee knew that this would take as long as it took. But she couldn't wait to get started with the editing. Her friends, envious of her whittled-down shape, had already put in their orders. She was losing weight while Meredith encouraged her to eat small and enjoy. Grande was out, pequeña in. Even her dentist was happy now that she had taken up chewing. Had she even tasted that burrito before? As for her stomach, no her abdominals—thanks to Pilates—they were shrinking, too. She still slipped up and referred to them as her stomach even though Meredith patiently explained to her that the stomach was a small, six-inch long sausage-shaped container located under her left breast. Lee frequently felt for it just to make sure that it stayed put and didn't expand.

"You know, Eve," said Lee. "In a way, they're at a disadvantage. They have to unlearn much of what their dance training and other exercise taught them about movement. Regular Janes and Joes like me don't have that baggage. I felt like a virgin my first time on the Reformer."

"Very true," Eve smiled. "Now let's hope that they can unlearn enough to get this video finished sometime before the end of the twentieth century."

Finally, the shoot was over, and then the editing completed. By the time the video copies were delivered, they realized that they had a hit. Pilates was building faster than they or anyone had anticipated. The Institute had emboldened more teachers to come out of hiding and identify their studios with the Pilates name. Teachers who had before taught only a few clients daily were now working all day everyday. More articles followed *Elle*'s lead starting a chain reaction. The media was lining up to report on this 'new', better yet, old exercise Method. Johanna studied the articles and saw the connection.

"Our overnight success has a lot to do with this celebrity name-dropping thing. For years, reporters were cautious about writing that some movies star or socialite was a client of this hairdresser or that stylist, but now it's open season," explained Johanna.

"Maybe we should send Princess Di a complimentary video. Isn't the obsession with her celebrity and how the tabloids get away with exposing her secrets a part of it?" asked Lee.

"Right. The media is on a celebrity roll. We are going to see a celebrity connection for everything. Lucky for us, too. Rob Flacher taught everyone in Hollywood Pilates, so we have many, many names for the press to drop."

"We can't get enough of our stars. We have to know their

foods, their skin care. Whatever they use and where and how they move their muscles. We know that they get the best, so it follows that we need to know their secrets," said Lee.

Johanna looked at Lee with a "wake up and smell the coffee" expression on her face.

"I shouldn't say anything because the media dropping celebrity names who love Pilates is working for us, but it is really crazy," explained Johanna. "I promise that this won't leave here, but stars who make $10 million bucks a movie shouldn't be our role models. They have staff, who have their own staff, to run their lives. Plus their own personal trainers and masseuses who travel with them. Private chefs who make delicious foods without any calories. Their own team of plastic surgeons, aestheticians, hairdressers, make-up artists, manicurist, stylists, so on. Why isn't the unreality of their situation obvious to bookkeepers, fast food workers, bank tellers, secretaries and everyone else who doesn't have unlimited time and money?"

"I haven't heard one word of this rant," Lee shouted. "My immediate decision, having just finished the article on the Flacher studio for the next Forum, is this: Do I list the names alphabetically, or begin with the biggest by star power? In a democratic spirit, I'd start with Jennifer Aniston, Denise Austen, George Balanchine, Drew Barrymore, Catherine Bell, the Princes of Brunei, Sonja Braga which could take up an entire page even in 9 point type or just cut   to the chase and go with the big wattage as in Julia Roberts, Madonna, Susan Sarandon, Glenn Close. Also, what about the dead ones? If we delete them, then George goes, and if he hadn't wandered into Joe's studio 50 years ago then it would have folded and there wouldn't be any Master teachers who later trained the stars, and we wouldn't have to figure out the best rating system," Lee finally exhaled before finishing with,

"Johanna, are you paying attention?"

8

THE MINI-REFORMER

"To those used to crunching and grunting, the Pilates method seems a gentle surprise. But this civilized system for stretching and strengthening muscles can transform your body."
—Lear's *Magazine*, 1994

Five weeks later, Lee was engulfed in boxes of the first Pilates Matwork video, *Working Out With Pilates.* Her staff, two high schoolers, spent their afternoons packing and shipping orders. She was ready to celebrate what they had accomplished. Johanna's thoughts were on the exploding Pilates market and what to do next. Training better teachers faster—circumventing years of apprenticeship—was obviously the next challenge. In the mainstream fitness world, certification was a weekend. Now that Pilates was getting so much publicity, aerobics teachers who had never been in a room with a Reformer were calling the Institute so they could get in on the latest big thing. Obviously apprenticing for years wasn't what they wanted to hear. Neither was relocating to Los Angeles or New York or now Santa Fe for a year of training. Johanna knew that to accelerate training and yet improve its quality required an affordable bridge.

She had already decided that an alliance with Kent Hemel, whose company crafted professional Reformers, was the place to build a bridge. Hemel's business was a $2000 Rolls Royce-quality Reformer with a four month wait. Confronted with a problem, she visualized a solution: a Mini-Reformer machine, a kind of a pre-Pilates professional tool, like Eve's Fundamentals. It should be affordable, a price point in the hundreds instead of thousands of dollars. It should be foldable and light so it could be shipped UPS with a video of the Reformer exercises. The Mini-Reformer would allow prospective teachers to learn the repertoire before going to a training studio for a few months to hone their teaching skills.

Immediately after Eve's workshop, she sought to convince Hemel that the Mini would lead to many more sales of the Grande. With the Mini, she pitched, there would be more trained teachers, which meant more studios opening and thus more professional apparatus sales. The Mini-Reformer was the key link to seeing his apparatus sales explode exponentially.

Kent's interest was piqued. The *Elle* article, Eve's successful workshop, and the huge New Mexican sky made anything seem possible. He left the next morning after making a commitment to build a prototype right away.

Ten months later, Johanna was again pacing the

small office. 'Delay, linger, and wait' was how she described it. Santa Fe speed—slow and stopped—drove her nuts. Laid back California style was just as bad. This disease of inaction was contagious. Kent's cautiousness, the purported explanation for chronic delays, felt more and more like a cover. Instead of a prototype from Kent, she received confidentiality agreements, letters of intent, and restatements of who was to do what and when. He was papering over the real issue—fear of risk. Johanna was by nature too much of a pragmatist to be a gambler. But trial and errors were part of any successful venture. Right? If mistakes happened, you just fixed them. Kent's development of a paper trail rather than a prototype was leading nowhere.

One day, after a particularly maddening phone call with Kent, Johanna hung up, spritzed herself with her ubiquitous Evian spray and said to Margaret: "Why can't he see that the tide is rising? We've got the boat, all we have to do is slide it out of its moorings."

"Why should he? He has been making Reformers since 1975. He is totally in control. He knows his customers, Pilates' studios, mostly in the West, and they wait patiently. Remember, a big part of Kent's business is crafting special order Reformers for movie star clients who buy them for their several residences. Often in special colors and personal detailing. The studios make a big commission when one of their clients wants to buy a Reformer. You know that we sold one this year to you know who and we made $500 just for a phone call. Dealing Reformers is much easier than slaving over a hot Reformer," Margaret said.

Johanna smiled at Margaret's choice of metaphor. She, like most dancers, had limited culinary skills. Trail mix, salads and yogurt sustained them. Their stoves never got hot. Their ovens were more likely to be used as storage for their old toe shoes than to cook a roast. While dancers did not labor strenuously in the kitchen, she thought, she knew of no other professionals that worked harder, but on their own terms and schedules. Corporate teamwork, Johanna's model, was unknown to them.

"We have the C words covered. Core. Control. Concentration. Centering. What's missing is Cooperation," Johanna said.

And confidence. She knew that Kent's coolness was in direct proportion to the Institute's growing influence. Johanna couldn't win him over even though she knew that an alliance would grow Pilates faster, weaken the trademark threat, and both organizations would benefit. She believed that one and one would be much more than two.

Thus, after a year of gridlock with Kent, Johanna was not able to share Lee's celebratory mood.   She had to have a prototype. Then one day, an answer appeared in the form of something Santa Fe had in abundance: over-educated craftsmen.

Randy Peterson, a science fiction writer supporting himself as a carpenter, phoned the Institute. Lee, impressed that a caller pronounced the name correctly, excitedly told Johanna about the call. Randy, having heard somewhat about Pilates, asked the cost of individual sessions. He followed up on Johanna's suggestion and showed up to observe a lesson before committing to a series. After observing a class, he scheduled a session and was hooked, but unfortunately was unable to finance his new passion. In true Santa Fe style, he offered to trade services. What did they need? Shelving, a table, another dressing room? All of them Johanna said. But first, a prototype.

A month later, Randy arrived in his workout gear with a wooden machine he'd built from Johanna's specs. It didn't fold well, and the ride was bumpy not gliding, but it was good enough for Johanna to execute her latest plan, contacting manufacturers of aerobic machines. She expected that it was going to be simple to convince them to make the Mini now that Pilates was the next big thing—because it was.

As Lee assembled photographs of the prototype and copies of recent articles to send to them, Johanna explained to her why this was just what they needed.

"Pilates won't stay a niche for long, so it is better for us to play with the big guys. They sell to the health clubs and spas. They've had 20 years of going from zero to billions and have to maintain that growth. We're giving them the next big thing. This is a tunnel into Fort Knox. Aerobics has peaked and we're up!" she said to Lee.

"Right, but some have already hedged their bets. They've branched into weight training machines. Try not to inform them that one Reformer can replace an entire circuit of 16 machines," Lee said, unconvinced by Johanna's unlimited optimism.

A month later Johanna was feeling their resistance. "I can't believe that a new product manager at a major fitness company has never heard about Pilates. Or even yoga. What am I missing here?" Johanna asked Lee.

"How about this guy doesn't care about looking smart. He only cares about being rich. You've just spent 40 minutes telling him everything about Pilates and why it is different. He now has all the ammunition he needs to undermine it and he hasn't had to use a single brain cell or even move a muscle," explained Lee.

"This is what I call 'Texas smart', playing dumb while calculating how you can undermine anything original. These are the same kids who didn't raise their hands in school,"said Johanna with disgust even though she had seen it before, executives working to kill something that they thought would threaten their existing businesses. The miracle of American capitalism had its dark side. Or maybe it was more mundane. Just a reflection of the Mickey Mouse behavior that passes for 'executive' decision making.

Then an unexpected break, or maybe a sign, occurred. Lee took a call from Will Cutler, head of exercsie equipment at Nortrax. Johanna's proposal had made it to his desk and he was intrigued. Why? His brother was in rehabilitation for a knee injury with a physical therapist who just happened to use a Reformer in her work.

"How do you pronounce it ?" he asked again.

"Puh-lah-teez," Lee told him. "Don't worry. Nobody gets it right at first."

"It's a mouthful," Will said. "But, my brother says it works. I took a look at what you sent over about your neat little machine. I don't know, I thought maybe there was something to the Pilaatees."

"There's a lot to it. I know you want to speak with Johanna Breyers. She's been doing it for decades."

During a long conversation, Johanna convinced Will

that there was indeed something to it. In fact, she said, it was the next big thing and convinced him that he owed it to his body and his company to check it out. Two weeks later, he flew in ready for a test drive. In the studio, the comparisons between the Reformer and the wooden Mini prototype would prove interesting. Will's six-foot frame with only a slight paunch lay on the floor between the two Reformers. He examined them closely.

"Springs," he said, looking up at Johanna with inquisitive eyes and a ready smile.

"Springs?"

"Springs," he said. He placed his hand on the Reformer's spring bar. "Now I can shrink this thing and get it to fold. I can reduce its weight so it's easy to ship." He leaned over the Mini-Reformer prototype and moved the carriage back and forth. "I can smooth out the action here, so there's no bump. What I can't do is manufacture it with springs."

Johanna and Margaret shared a worried look. Spring resistance worked with the body's natural mechanics. Springs equal Pilates.

"Springs look simple," he said. "But trust me, there's nothing more complex than manufacturing a perfect spring.

The dud ratio is high. They're also expensive, heavy, and difficult to ship." He gestured toward the Cadillac and the original Reformer. "I'm not surprised these things cost what they do."

"We've got our own stories," said Johanna. "We sell our members, Pilates teachers, replacement springs for their Reformers. They arrive here in giant barrels that look like a pit of snakes! Worse, almost 20 percent of them are no good."

Will shook his head. "Stay away from springs. They're bad news."

Johanna's perfectly-aligned body stiffened against Will's negativity, but she wasn't ready to give up on her Mini-Reformer.

Thankfully, neither was he.

"Bungees," he said. "Cheap, light, easy to work with."

An expression of relief spread across Johanna's face. "I knew I liked you, Will. I knew you didn't fly all the way out here just to tell us this couldn't work."

"Actually," he said. "I would have come out here just to see Santa Fe. So," he clapped his hands together jovially. "Where can I take you ladies for dinner tonight? Let's have a Pulatees celebration. Did I say that right?"

And for the first time since they started the Institute, Johanna agreed it was time to celebrate, now that the pieces were falling into place. The deal with Nortrax would put the Institute on the map. Simultaneously, publicity was building—a *Dallas Morning News* article had set the phones on fire. The video was so popular that a major fitness catalogue had agreed to offer it, and workshops and certification courses were filling. Pilates was on the verge of breaking out and the Nortrax deal was proof of it. Johanna wanted to let the growing Pilates community know that they had engineered this success.

"Why not announce our deal with Nortrax?" she asked, when Margaret made it clear she disagreed and was totally against it.

"What's the worst that could happen?" Johanna asked her partner.

They'd find that out soon enough.

9

THE PROTOTYPE

"The endless search for the best, hardest, most effec-tive, cheapest, Type-A one-stop workout has brought us full circle to a machine from the 1920s—the Pilates Reformer."

— City Sports, 1991

Margaret loved all the Pilates apparatus, even the Spine Corrector, but the Reformer was her special friend. She had logged thousands of Reformer hours in the 20 years since Eve had rehabilitated her back after a career-ending dance injury. Its polished blonde wood, thick leather cushioning, and steel springs were a kind of salvation. She looked forward to being on a Reformer, the way most people felt about lying down on a massage table.

So as Will Cutler guided them through Nortrax's Milwaukee campus one grey September afternoon to the room where he was to present his prototype of the Mini-Reformer, she tried to share in his excitement. But upon viewing the miniscule apparatus lying on the grey-carpeted floor in the drab windowless room, her disappointment was hard to hide.

"It looks like a luggage cart," she whispered to Johanna.

Will hovered over the prototype, palms upturned like a magician revealing the white rabbit from his black hat. "So," he said. "Margaret, Johanna, tell me the truth. What do you think?"

Not knowing what to say she glanced at Johanna in an attempt to gauge her reaction. She revealed nothing but curiosity.

"I don't know, Will," Johanna said. "Let's see it in action."

She slipped off her three-inch tan suede pumps and lay down on the beige plastic carriage. Pressing her stocking feet against the foot bar, she pushed back to test the sliding action . "Hmm," she said.

"Smooth, isn't it?" Will couldn't stop smiling. Johanna sat up and fooled with the headrest. "Is it adjustable?"

Will sprung into action to drop it down to the flat position. Standing up, Johanna placed her hands on the foot bar, stepped back onto the carriage and lifted herself into an Arabesque.

"You know," Johanna said. "It's quite solid."

"Exactly," Will said. "It's more stable because it sits

on the floor instead of on four legs."

Johanna pushed back on the carriage again. "It doesn't slide quite as smoothly without the ball bearings."

"But," Will said. "It weighs only 50 pounds. $49.95 for UPS. Forget the standard $300 for truck delivery."

From her inverted position, Johanna laughed. "I like that. Margaret, why don't you give it a try?"

While Johanna discussed metal choices and colors, Margaret performed her usual routine. The Mini was so small she was reluctant to trust it with her weight, but after the first six moves, she sensed its solidness. "You're right that it's not as smooth as the professional one," she said.

"No," Johanna said. "But remember, the people using this won't be comparing it to the original." "True," she conceded, concentrating on the movement. It wasn't exactly the same, but it felt appropriate. Adjusting the head rest, she tried Short Spine. This seemed OK. The real test, however, she concluded, couldn't be done here and now. She needed more time alone with this machine to find out whether bungees really worked.

"Can I drop this down?" she asked.

"Yep." Will crouched and fingered a bolt on the foot bar." He pulled it backwards. Margaret ran through one more test.

Will backed up to give her room to move. "I've got a couple more changes I want to make," he said. "Jesus." He cringed as he watched Margaret descend into a full split with arms raised overhead. "None of our simulators could do that."

She laughed. A full split always impressed people. "You know," she said stepping off the machine. "The carriage does slide smoothly."

"And if not," Will said. "We'll ship it with a can of WD-40."

"Alright," Johanna said. "Let's see how it folds."

Will bent down to help, but Johanna waved him off.

"No, no," she said. "I want to see if a size 6 woman can do this. That's our market."

Johanna stared at the apparatus for a moment to figure out how to fold it then easily collapsed it and stood it on its two wheels. "Later," she said, heading for the door.

"I'll send you a bill," Will said. "For 400 dollars."

Johanna smiled and stopped with the Mini-Reformer in tow. "I like the sound of that number. Gosh it's light.   Is $400 the right price?"

"That's what management says. Brastic thinks that's a good price point for a stretching machine."

James Brastic was the President of Nortrax. Johanna had spoken to him by telephone only.

Johanna's face couldn't mask her annoyance. "It's a lot more than stretching," she said. "This is about balancing the body."

Will laughed a full, hearty laugh. "Whatever you do," he said. "Don't use those words with Brastic. Just tell him it's a stretching machine."

"But Will..." Johanna said.

"I know, I know," he interrupted. "But if Brastic can't understand it, his marketing people won't either. You've got to keep things simple. You can't sell a machine on the idea that it does hundreds of things."

"Thousands actually," Johanna said. "It trains strength, flexibility, balance, coordination, control, concentration, proprioception. The moves are practically unlimited. The only limits are your imagination."

"Don't make it complicated. You'll lose them."

"It's complex," Johanna said. "Not complicated. That's the beauty of Pilates. That's what gives it its depth. It's just like the human body. Elegantly simple yet complex."

Will smiled at Johanna. "I understand that. But I'm an engineer. Brastic and his money guys like simple because it sells. To them, a machine that lets you walk in place is some kind of miracle because anyone can do it."

Johanna looked at her watch. "Well," she said. "Thanks for the tip. It will be hard for us to 'Keep It Simple Stupid' but at least we've been warned. We've got 30 minutes before our meeting with Brastic. Time to stretch our bodies and shrink our brains."

"Just don't oversell Pilates and we will get this little beauty to market," Will said.

They met Brastic for the first time in his expansive corner office which was paneled in dark wood with floor-to-ceiling windows. Sitting in matching black leather and chrome chairs around an oval table, Brastic was flanked by two men in grey suits. Bert and Ernie she decided because their names were lost as soon as they were introduced as

Nortrax's in-house counsel.   Brastic was not smiling.

"Things have changed," he said. Brastic, overweight and not the picture of health, loomed over them even when seated. His dark blue suit covered him like an oversized tent.

"Changed?" Johanna said.

He nodded gravely. "You see we're not interested in getting involved in a trademark lawsuit, Johanna. I wish you'd told us about this before we invested time and money building a prototype."

"There's no trademark on the name Reformer. And we have trademarked Mini-Reformer, so what's the problem?" Johanna said icily.

"But there is on the name 'Pilates' and this is a Pilates machine."

Brastic leaned back in his chair and glanced at the dark haired lawyer on his right. Call him Ernie, whatever.

Ernie was shaking his head. "I'm afraid I have to counsel against it," he said. "This product puts us at risk."

"A patent, not a trademark, is what we need for this machine," Johanna bristled.

Brastic placed his bear-like hands on the polished mahogany table and hunched over with the full weight of his bulk. "We are not worried about patents. What good is a Pilates machine if you can't say Pilates?"

The tension in Johanna's face was evident.

"Jim," Margaret interrupted. "Our own Eve Gentry was one of Joe's students. Roberta has no more right to the name than she does. Eve has used the name for decades. Lots of people use the name. Studios specifically use it."

The other lawyer, 'Bert,' chuckled derisively. "You don't understand how these things work. I'm sorry. What was your name?"

"Margaret," she responded sternly to his condescending tone.

"You see, Margaret," he said. "A product needs to be branded and the brand is Pilates. It doesn't make any difference whether the trademark claim ultimately holds up in court. A decision on something like that could take many years. In the meantime, we can't use it."

"We have gotten this far without using the name," Johanna said sharply. "We're calling it the Mini-Reformer. Saying it is based on exercises developed by Joseph Pilates."

Brastic sucked his teeth as he contemplated the idea then shook his head. "Too complicated. Look, that woman in New York owns the name and we don't. Period."

Johanna and Margaret shared a look.

"Jim," Johanna said. "This is the future of fitness. You saw all the articles I sent you. Everyone is talking about Pilates."

Unaware that she was ensnaring herself in his own trap, Johanna kept fighting. "But people don't know whether Pilates is a man, a machine, or a method. It's the concept they're interested in. There's no trademark on that."

"Look, look," he said. "I'm sorry to drag you ladies all the way up here. It's a nice little machine. It really is. But we're going to have to pass."

Johanna's breathing intensified but her face remained calm as she stared at Brastic. "A phone call?" she said.

Brastic furrowed his already wrinkled forehead. "Excuse me?"

Johanna took hold of her small alligator purse and pushed her chair away from the table. "You couldn't have phoned us about this before we flew out here?" She was on her feet now.

"And miss the chance to meet you in person?" Brastic said. His grin was wide and forced. "No, seriously, ladies. We only learned about this yesterday." He turned to Bert. "What was that guy's name?"

Bert checked a stack of papers on the table in front of him. "Steve Gross," he said. "He even included a copy of your Pilates Forum in which you announced our manufacturing partnership. We received a cease and desist by fax from Gross's lawyer this morning around 9:30."

Johanna looked at the clock. It was 12:40pm. "And in that amount of time you decided to kill the deal?"

Brastic smiled smugly. "We move fast around here."

Clearly, at this point, Johanna sensed they were outmatched. She would be able to think this through later with a bit of pacing. No way was she leaving with the insinuation that she had brought in a compromised product. And no way was she leaving without getting them to give her the prototype.

Shouldering her handbag, Johanna extended her hand to Brastic and concluded with, "But the prototype is our design. And the contract that we both signed makes it clear that we don't own the name Pilates. You knew that going in. Thus, we own the prototype we just reviewed with Will.

"Touché." he said. "Ladies, we will ship it to Santa Fe. Aren't you glad we didn't phone you?"

Johanna headed to the door. "Yes and no," she said.

Once they arrived at the elevator door, Johanna pressed the down button and stared into the glass doors at their slightly distorted reflections. The doors opened and they stepped into the empty elevator.

"You know they didn't invent their best-selling aerobics machine," Johanna said. "They just marketed it and rode the aerobics craze."

"Your point?" snapped Margaret, showing fatigue.

The elevator moved slowly and silently down the twelve flights.

"Their numbers are way down now. They killed this deal because Pilates intimidates them—too new—too complicated. This isn't about the trademark."

The elevator doors opened and they stepped into the sober marble lobby. Outside in the parking lot their rented white Ford sedan sat waiting. It was a dull grey day with a chill in the air.

"I don't know Johanna," Margaret said. "Maybe they're not using the trademark to kill the deal. Maybe they are. But one thing is certain—that trademark is a real problem. We're going to have to deal with it."

It was a silent drive back to the airport. Since the lunch with Nortrax's marketing people had been abruptly cancelled, they arrived three hours early for their flight. Margaret, their designated driver, pulled the car into an empty slot, turned off the engine and just stared ahead for a moment wondering if the whole enterprise had been a waste of time. Her mind wandered. All she could think about was the energy they had poured into the Institute, building the reputation of a brand for someone else's benefit. It was pointless to feign surprise that the trademark had surfaced. It had been circling like a shark from the very beginning. Now it had finally taken a bite. All they had done was to rush ahead ignoring every ominous sign as they hurried to reach Johanna's goal to put Pilates on the map.

"Let's hurry," Johanna said. "Maybe we can catch an earlier flight."

10

LAWSUIT

"The equipment used in Pilates looks nothing like the machines found in gyms. It includes contraptions like the Cadillac, a four-poster frame with straps and springs hanging from it, and the Universal Reformer, a bedlike apparatus with sliding parts."
—**Albuquerque Journal, 1993**

Johanna spent the next few weeks digging through legal documents, learning about trademarks and looking for a patent lawyer.   Sometimes laughing at the latest lawyer joke: "What's ten thousand lawyers at the bottom of the ocean?" Answer: "A pretty good start." At other times lamenting that her only pertinent next move was the LSATs. The futility of the situation hit hard. Pilates was morphing from a tiny cult to a niche in the fitness world. They deserved, had earned really, a piece of the pie. The perfect Pilates product was sitting on a Sautillo floor in Santa Fe, dead in the water.

Margaret was drifting. Product development was no longer worth her energy. Her withdrawal added to the already tense atmosphere. A dancer first, her natural inclination was to go inward. She was not equipped for the battle that loomed ahead. Johanna was anxious, but too committed to admit that she might have miscalculated. Margaret watched as Johanna brushed off each obstacle wondering if anything ever cost her, or did she simply relished the sport. Soon enough they would discover they had misread more than each other's personalities.

Johanna charged forward with the Mini-Reformer. Figuring out how to sell it without the P word could come later. Running the Institute, writing the Forum, getting new publicity, helping studio members get started, even working on other products became secondary. Legal bills began to escalate. Lee was also feeling the drain. She no longer enjoyed watching the Certification students trying to perfect the advanced exercises like Control Balance into Arabesque. Her own Pilates goals, what she wanted as her personal best, were now unimportant. Johanna spent most days talking to lawyers who were 'helping' them do battle. The trademark which had previously been questioned by their legal experts was now seemingly golden. Meanwhile Johanna neglected her body and distanced herself from the exercises she had loved. It was as if she couldn't bear to get too close and feel the passion.

Fortunately, Margaret kept the Institute going by taking on more clients and more teacher training. She was now almost exclusively in the downstairs studio.

Then one unusually quiet morning, she surprised Lee with a rare appearance in the office. "Did Thea call?

She's always on time. She missed last week and now she's ten minutes late today."

"Jeez, I am sorry," Lee said. "I completely forgot."

Johanna turned and said, "Forgot what? You look like you've seen an alien."

Lee pushed away from the Mac and spun around to face both of them. "Thea did call, Margaret. I'm so sorry. I completely forgot to tell you. She won't be coming in for a while. She's just been diagnosed with breast cancer. She called this morning right before you came in. I got stuck on the phone...then I just...I'm soooo sorry."

Margaret slumped against a file cabinet. She'd been training Thea Van Dyke for six years.

"Alright," Johanna said trying to turn the bad news into a positive. "This is a sign that we should all get mammograms. Lee, set up appointments for all three of us at Santa Fe Radiology."

Downstairs, the door opened and someone entered.

"Eve?" Lee called down.

"Hello," a man's gravely voice said. "I'm looking for

Johanna Breyers."

"Up here," Johanna said. "Take the stairs on the right." A fifty-ish, balding man with a thin ponytail and a less than crisp blue suit appeared at the top of the stairs carrying a battered nylon briefcase. "Johanna Breyers?" he said, out of breath, coughing.

"Right here," Johanna said.

He squeezed between Lee and the skeleton, plopped his briefcase on the Mission table, popped open the two locks and pulled out a manila envelope and a piece of white paper. "Sign here," he said.

Johanna regarded him as if he were a cockroach standing on top of her sandwich. These aging hippie types with their rusting cars full of bumper stickers and dog hair were just another reminder she was not living in her proper milieu. This was something she found herself pondering more and more often from the sanctuary of her Italian couch.

"What am I signing?"

"You are being served, courtesy of Black and Black, Attorneys at Law."

Johanna took the manila envelope from his hands and

opened it. Glistening with excreted sweat, the man offered the piece of paper up to her. "You MUST sign these." He reeked of all things she wanted to know nothing about: Echinecea, kelp, cedar, smudge sticks, blue/green algae, and anti-oxidants.

Johanna took the piece of paper from him and speed-read it. He handed her his pen. "Oh, please," she murmured while retrieving her own pen from her handbag. She signed the paper quickly.

"Thank you," the man said. "Whatever is going on downstairs looks pretty awesome, ladies. Have a great day!"

Johanna ripped into the envelope and tore it open.

"We're being sued for trademark infringement." Johanna flipped through the pages, her eyes zigzagging at light speed. She kept reading then stopped abruptly.

"Oh, my God. That piece of shit. He's suing me personally, too."

The shark was still circling. It was taking another bite, this time a really big one.

11

PATENTS

"These days, Pilates is hot with the 'I-used-to-do-aer-obics-but-now-it-hurts-too-much' baby boomers as a form of conditioning."
—Yoga Journal, 1995

Margaret drove Johanna's car south on Interstate 285 to Albuquerque. Since patent lawyers in New Mexico cluster around the two national laboratories, the choice had been either there or Los Alamos. For Eastern transplants like Johanna, neither place was worth visiting. Albuquerque, the largest city in the state and home to Sandia National Laboratory, was short on charm, long on fast-food franchises, and artless 'sky' scrapers—not hard when you start at fifty-five hundred feet.

They arrived on time at the tallest building downtown and took the elevator to the twelfth floor offices of Grey, Grise, & Gris, Attorneys at Law. A neatly dressed woman, Pilar, escorted them down a long corridor. Margaret noted that the right side teemed with secretary stations. Commercial photos of gaily dressed 4-year-olds, soccer trophies, special occasion plants wrapped in foil, several hundred themed coffee mugs, and other bric-a-brac of life lived somewhere else, cluttered, or depending on one's perspective, breathed life into the uniform space. Along the left of the corridor, small windowed offices emitted the uneven pitch of men in suits taking calls.

Randall Whitehorpe, on the phone himself, waved them in. He pointed to two chairs, repeated "Tuesday, Tuesday" several times and finished the call. He then rose to shake hands.

"Soda? Coffee?" he inquired. "Did Pilar offer you anything?"

"No, thanks," Johanna said. "We're fine."

Whitethorpe sat down, and picked up his phone quickly. "Pilar, Sheridan promised Tuesday. Notify the lab." While speaking he opened a thick manila file and pulled out its contents. Johanna recognized right away the copies of Pilates articles she had sent him.

"Okay," he said. "Pee-lotz, right? The multi-reformer. Where's that picture you sent me?"

He rifled through the pages in the manila file. His phone rang. Wisely, he didn't take the call.

"Mini-Reformer," Johanna corrected, "And it's

pronounced Puh-lah-teez."

Whitethorpe nodded. "Never tried it. Do either of you play tennis? Now that's great exercise."

Johanna shifted her handbag. Tennis was not great exercise. Fun? Yes. Social? Yes. Back East it still offered some status. But, like all one sided-sports, imbalances or worse injuries often followed. Tennis 'exercise' didn't deliver better bodies.

"Well, between the tennis elbow clients and the torn ACLs, we can't recommend tennis for body conditioning," Johanna said.

"Here we are," Whitethorpe said and placed Johanna's drawing of the Mini-Reformer on the desk.

"According to a lawyer friend of mine," Johanna said. "We need to choose between a design patent and a functional patent. I know functional patents are more expensive and take longer to get but we need to know if—"

Whitethorpe interrupted, shaking his head and slumping back right on his sacrum in his high-backed leather chair. Johanna knew he would find his back hurting if he kept that up. "First thing I tell new clients is never trust what lawyer friends tell you. Patent law is complicated.

That's why you're here."

Whitethorpe was good-looking, blond, with overly developed pectorals and biceps. No point in bringing up Pilates balanced body philosophy with him.

Glancing at his black phone where a red indicator light had turned to green, he held up a finger. "Give me a sec." He picked up the receiver and spun his chair away. "Tuesday, that's it," he said.

"How much will this cost?" Margaret whispered to Johanna.

"It's by the hour. We teach him everything we know about Pilates. Then he charges us for it."

"Now," Whitethorpe said. He spun around and hung up the phone. "Now let me ask you girls a question." Whitethorpe was a good 10 years younger than both 'girls.' He shuffled through the file for another sheet of paper. "Why are you seeking a patent on this thing? The original patent expired in the forties."

Johanna leaned forward and glanced at the photograph Whitethorpe held of Joe Pilates standing by his Reformer. "This is a different design," she said. "What we're patenting is the device which allows it to fold."

Whitethorpe placed the photo of Joe face down on his desk and pulled out another drawing of a machine she'd never seen before. "That hinge is already in use," he said.

"Not on a Reformer," Johanna said. "What distinguishes our machine is the way that it folds."

Whitethorpe was unimpressed. "For this small machine, I don't think you want to get involved with a functional patent. We should, although, be able to knock out a design patent for you in no time. Save you some money. But don't tell my partners I said that." His smile revealed large white teeth.

"But anyone could just redesign some aesthetics and we would have nothing," Johanna said. "Are you sure this is the way to go?"

"Absolutely," he said. "I'll have Pilar fax over my standard retainer agreement this afternoon." He began to stand as the phone rang, a cue that he needed to attend to important business.

"We can find our way out," Johanna murmured as they passed a secretary carrying a large box of donuts.

The Sandia mountain range drifted into the East as Margaret sped in Johanna's racing green-colored Miata back to Santa Fe. The sky began its long descent from azure to a lighter blue palette. The tacky urban sprawl of Albuquerque receded as the road flattened out before them. Pinon trees dotted the hills far to the horizon. The scenery, so familiar and peaceful, should have soothed Margaret's jostled nerves. Instead, she felt achy. That familiar 'coming down with something' feeling. Tired. Throat tight. Something wrong.

As they drove silently through the rolling landscape, Margaret wondered if they were already in too deep. Everything they were trying to create just seemed to produce another headache. What was that phrase? "Trouble was her middle name." Bad luck and bad timing had diminished her previous enthusiasm. She felt drained, pretty much all the time.

"It's amazing how much ego a guy can squeeze out of a law degree and an engineering background," Johanna said, puncturing the silence. "They're not even inventors. They're just facilitators. Why would you spend so much time in school just to circumvent other people's inventions? I just don't get it."

"I don't know," Margaret said. "But I particularly

enjoyed the way he called us 'girls'."

"That wouldn't happen in New York," Johanna said. "He would have to pretend to view us as equals even if he thinks we are just wasting his time with our wimpy little exercise machine. In a macho culture, even Anglos feel safe giving in to their suppressed chauvinism."

"It's not just chauvinism, though," Margaret said. "There is so much resistance to Pilates itself."

"It's all or nothing," Johanna concurred. " Everyone hates it except for the people who love it. Why?"

"People are insecure, especially in their bodies."

"Terminally insecure is what it looks like. Paying attention to your body is healthy. Obsessing about every figure fault is crazy. People choose mindless exercises so they can distance themselves from their bodies when they could be doing Pilates and focusing on their alignment and how they move and getting their bodies to function better."

Margaret looked pained. "Maybe our exercise method is really only for a select few. You know that is what the Advisors feel. They are ambivalent about putting it out there. They are worried that people will hurt themselves."

"We believe that Pilates is the best exercise which means that all bodies will benefit. I bet in 10 years some study will prove that complex movement, such as Pilates, improves brain function. We've got an aging population. Fitness has been about thin thighs and cute butts. But in a few years, we will have to deal with senior moments and worn out joints. For right now we've got someone working on the patent. Now all we need is someone to build the thing."

Margaret kept her eyes on the blacktop as another billboard begged her to stay in "Old Town" somewhere. In 10 years, would she feel any better, she asked herself?

"New Mexico is crawling with engineers," Johanna said as ever rallying. "Let's find some guy who needs a rest from high-tech and defense work."

To Johanna, it was as simple as that. If you want to sell a Mini-Reformer, you build it yourself. Patent issues, trademark issues, manufacturing contracts—to Johanna, these were minor details. Lemons to lemonade.

"Margaret," she said. "Stop worrying so much. It'll give you wrinkles."

She laughed. "I'm not like you, Johanna."

"Nobody's like me," she said.

That may have been the understatement of the century.

"Look," Johanna said. "My friend Dianne is an entre-preneur who built a terrific skin care business. She described the process as: you start with an idea. That's all. It is as if you were at the bottom of a pit. You work and work and gradually you crawl your way up. Then just as your hand reaches over the top of the ledge, someone or something knocks you back down."

"Is that supposed to be encouraging?"

"Yes," she said. "It means we're doing something right. These are normal obstacles. If we slow down now we will lose our lead."

Slowing down at La Bahada, skid marks of car acci-dents from long ago caught Margaret's peripheral vision. All she wanted now was to slow down to a stop. A year ago, she had been a Pilates teacher, a good one. Life was simple. Now she was part of something that seemed to be spiraling out of control. She'd never been sued before, couldn't brush it off the way Johanna did. And now the Institute was col-lecting lawyers—trademark lawyers, litigators, and patent lawyers. She didn't understand their advice or the contracts and letters she put her signature on all too frequently.

As the burning terrain of the desert whipped past

the car windows, they sped towards Santa Fe and the Pilates Institute. All she could think about was slamming on the brakes and bringing it all to a screeching halt.

12

EVE GENTRY

"First and foremost, Pilates is about posture. That's probably why such famous dancers as Eve Gentry and Martha Graham flocked to Joseph Pilates' New York studio when he brought his invention from Germany in 1926."
—Cooking Light Magazine, 1995

There was heaviness in the air when Margaret arrived at the studio the following day. It was just past nine and she had less than an hour to prepare for a new client with whiplash. Climbing the stairs to the office, she noticed there was not the usual sound of Lee typing. Was she the first to arrive? At the top of the stairs, she heard Johanna's unusually hushed voice talking on the phone.

Lee was sitting in front of the Mac without any show of activity. Her tear-stained face was the first hint that something was terribly wrong.

"Alright," Johanna said. "Thanks for calling, Jessica. If there's anything we can do at this time, please let us know. Good-bye."

She hung up and looked at Margaret.

"Don't tell me," Margaret said.

"That was Jessica. She called for you, of course."

"Is Eve?.." Margaret was unable to finish the sentence.

Lee got up from the Mac and put her arm around Margaret's waist. "I'm so sorry, Margaret."

"She died in her sleep," Johanna said. "No pain. No suffering."

Margaret dropped her blue canvas shoulder bag to the floor and collapsed into a chair. "How?" she said.

"Stroke," Johanna said, blinking back her tears. She placed her elbows on the table and dropped her head into her hands. Another death, she whispered to herself.

The following Sunday, Margaret stood at a podium looking out into the solemn crowd at Amelia White Park. Santa Fe society, gathered under a pergola of vine-covered aspen latillas, had come together for Eve's memorial service. Friends from the dance community, clients, artists, politicians, even some of Eve's former students from New York, were there to pay tribute. Margaret was proud to see that the large crowd filled every inch of the shaded area and spilled out into the bright sunlight. The setting, one of Santa Fe's most beautiful, sat on a wide open knoll rising above the low gentle curves of Santa Fe's historic eastside. The 360 degree vista reached forever into the ethereal space where the Sangres, Jemez and the Sandia Mountain Ranges surrounded the city.

"Just five years ago," Margaret spoke into the microphone. "Eve was honored with the title of Santa Fe Living Treasure. The award described her as *The Embodiment of Creative Energy*. What a perfect description of the woman who mentored so many of us here today. From childhood, Eve had a need to dance as her means of expression. Her discipline, her commitment and her natural born gifts propelled her to the position of principal performer with the Hanya Holm Company and a choreographer for her own company. Right up to the time of her death, Eve continued to teach and to share her knowledge. And, as many of you in the audience know, even at 84, she made people half her age look clumsy. She was immensely talented and graceful both in body and in spirit."

She stopped briefly as the audience nodded in agreement.

"Many of you here today know that Eve began studying Pilates with Joe in the forties and has continued to explore and evolve his Method, particularly in the past few years. Never holding back, she taught and mentored me with her unique, finely tuned instinct of how the body worked. By remembering Eve, we can keep her wisdom alive to educate another generation. Thank you."

After Eve's niece and three other Living Treasure honorees spoke about their memories of Eve, the large crowd gathered to drink Eve's favorite punch at the reception. Stephanie Pearl, a student of Eve's who had attended the Institute's first workshop, eyeballed Margaret standing by the refreshments and took her aside to speak privately.

"How are you doing?" she said.

Margaret took a deep breath, straightening her skirt. "Okay. I'm going to miss her terribly."

"We all will. All of her students will feel the loss. And the Institute? How will you manage? I heard that you have received a legal action. Is this a trademark infringement lawsuit?"

"I guess that is the actual terminology. We are going to be okay, though."

"I heard Johanna was sued personally."

"Why don't you ask her?" Margaret replied with

obvious annoyance at the intrusion of Pilates business at Eve's service.

Here they were, gathered to celebrate Eve's life and the practice she believed in, and the Pilates trademark mess was dirtying the ground under the pergola. Although Eve's fellow Pilates teachers, Joe's original students, were too old to make the trip, one had made her presence known in Santa Fe and elsewhere, without showing up or leaving New York. Roberta and her partner, Steve Gross, had peppered the Pilates community with cease and desist letters.

"Hi, Johanna, how are you?" Stephanie asked Johanna, who had joined them.

"Sad, of course, but at least she lived her life just as she wanted," she remarked.

'Yes she did. Don't we all wish for that? I haven't. I don't know what I'll do," Stephanie said. "I'm 68 and I need to plan for retirement. I love the Pilates work, but my mind is being eaten up with business worries even though my Albuquerque studio is busy for the first time since I started teaching 15 years ago. Do we stop using the name?"

"No," Johanna said with absolute determination. "And, yes, we have some serious concerns now. We have the papers to prove it. They have hired a proper trademark lawyer instead of using Steve's sister. Supposedly, he paid 10 grand for the mark. Bought it from its last failed owner, the guy who owned the Pilates Studio from 1986 until it went bust in 1988. Talk about a going-out-of-business sale."

"You think that is too little?" Stephanie said, her face fogging over.

"Too little?! It's like buying a real Rolex for twenty bucks! Valuable, legitimate trademarks are worth millions. He's already spent more on legal fees than he paid for it."

Stephanie looked at them anxiously. "So do we stop using it?"

"No," Johanna said. "Someone is going to find out if that trademark holds up in court. We know that the Pilates name was used before and after its registration. And even if it passes the registration test, has it been protected? Plus the name gets more generic each day. Excuse me for this legal diatribe, but I feel as if I could hang out my lawyer shingle, I have spent so much time on this. My assessment is that it will be cancelled. The question is when. And also how much will these legal manipulations cost? What will it cost us all personally to live through this nightmare?"

"But what do I do until then?" Stephanie said. "These letters keep coming. Why are they picking on me anyway? Letters aren't arriving to every Pilates studio. Only some. I've heard the ones trained by Roberta have been left alone."

"You're right. Her groupies are getting a free ride. I just heard that a studio in New York that doesn't use the name, but wasn't trained by Roberta, has been sued for "unfair competition." So not using the word is not protection either. Maybe I should have listened to Katherine Grey. She trained with Joe and ran his studio at Bendels. When we started the Institute, she told me the name was a jinx. I don't know what to tell you to do."

A tall Native American man in dark grey shirt with a long black ponytail called over to Johanna who excused herself to talk to him. After she left, Margaret continued, "I don't know what to say, Stephanie, I don't know how this will play out. But I don't have Johanna's steel gut. I'm feeling it," said Margaret as she instinctively covered her stomach with her right hand.

"What would Eve say?"

"She'd tell us to move forward," Margaret said. "She didn't believe Pilates was something you owned. It was something you did, something you were. But, fortunately. she was never sued. If only Joe were still alive. I never knew him, but I don't think that Joe would have protected his-work with lawyers."

Stephanie smiled and took a sip of her punch. Behind her, Johanna was beckoning energetically.

"Excuse me," Margaret said and walked over to Johanna, who handed her a business card. "Jim Whitehorse," she said. "That guy over there." She pointed to the fifty-ish Native American man she'd just been speaking with.

Margaret nodded. "What about him?"

"He runs Lagune Industries. You know them, right?"

She shrugged.

"Of course you know them," Johanna said. "Native American company. Owned and operated by one of the pueblos. They were written up in The *New Mexican*. They made Humvee parts during Desert Storm."

"Oh right," she lied. Just then Jim looked at them, nodded respectfully and walked over.

"Jim, Meet Margaret Holmes. She's my partner at the Institute."

Jim extended his hand. "Nice to meet you, Margaret. I'm sorry for your loss. Fifteen years ago I was blessed with an opportunity to see Eve perform at the Opera. I didn't know her age until you mentioned it today. She was almost 70 when I saw her dancing. She was amazing."

Johanna nodded for him to continue.

"Margaret, Johanna and I have been talking about the nature of your business. Your Mini-Reformer interests me. Johanna spoke of your troubles with Nortrax. Your company must not be familiar with a current trend: Think Globally—Act Locally. We are based right here in New Mexico. But this is not the time for business talk."

Margaret and Johanna stood in silence.

He looked directly at Johanna. "May I phone you on Monday?" he asked.

"You'll probably hear from her tonight," Margaret said, feeling her way out of the day's sadness. "Johanna's mind doesn't take time off."

Jim smiled. "I think if we can handle Desert Storm, we can handle a piece of exercise equipment for Miss Johanna here." He nodded politely. "Look forward to hearing from you both."

Jim began weaving himself back through the crowd.

Margaret noted the late afternoon sun was setting on another day. In this, she found solace.

Part 2
The Middle Years 1996-1999

" More and more people are discovering Pilates to tone and firm the body like nothing else can. Although new to most, Pilates is a 70-year-old body conditioning technique that utilizes unique equipment.   The PhysicalMind Institute...is a one stop source for teacher training, equipment and videos..."

—American Fitness, 1997

13

JOHANNA

"'Core' muscles: The hottest alternative fitness sub-cult is Pilates. This German-imported strength and flexibility method focuses on 'core' muscles and proper body alignment."
—Newsweek Magazine, 1995

As Johanna was zipping up the cover on her Wilson racket, she heard a familiar baritone and turned to see Brendon McKenzie and Al Langley approach the adjacent tennis court. She remembered them as half of Dan's regular Tuesday doubles match. Not stopping to say hello and then have to meet Dan's replacement, she left the court and walked quickly to the clubhouse lawn. She sat down to rest, took off her steamy tennis shoes and socks and let her feet snuggle in the damp, imported Kentucky bluegrass. Her mind roamed back to her previous life in New York where she fit in, where she was comfortable. There amid the turmoil, noise, and energy of her home city, were friends who could finish her sentences, argue with her, watch her back, and stand by her side. In a sense, her best friend, Dan, her husband who understood her, remained there too.

Coming to Santa Fe had carried a hope that rest and space

and sunlight would help Dan. What they hadn't intuited was his rapid decline and their life falling apart so quickly. She had called it what it was, a gamble, but figured the dream would fade, if at all, in drips and drabs, like real dreams do. Dan's disease took several years to take hold of both their lives. His death, her aloneness, their sons away at school in the East, had taken too much. She should have gone back to New York, but when she didn't leave immediately, she found herself immobilized with grief. And overwhelmed with her responsibilities. A year later, she convinced herself that starting the Institute would be a way for her to find herself. Now this Institute had become her trap. She felt increasingly lost, wanting to get out of Dodge, but she couldn't afford to. It was so true, dammit, that cashing out of Manhattan is a one way ticket. She didn't hate Santa Fe. How could anyone not fall for its beauty? She should have been able to breathe in these wide-open spaces. But instead, with its perfect weather and natural ease, Santa Fe had ruined her dinner without offering up any real nourishment.

She lay back on the grass, looked up at the immense sky, and thought about what sage business advice Dan would offer now that she had gotten herself into so much trouble. She now knew that she had rushed to start the Institute far too quickly. If Dan were still here, he would have supported her instincts about Pilates' potential, but tempered her need for speed. He would have cautioned her about being first, the sentential canary for the Pilates industry. He wouldn't have stopped her, but he would have prepared her for the predictable problems to come. '*Johanna*,' he would have reminded her, '*the first ones out of the gate make all the obvious mistakes.*' He would have known the length of the race.

With Dan still across the table, there would have been more research into potential trademark conflicts, and her arrangements with Eve and Margaret would be less amorphous. The loss of her long-time primary partner had left her vulnerable to rushing to find new connections. Now, swimming upstream in molasses, she had no one on her side, no one to help her fight back. She could quit, but that might not solve anything except saving whatever money she had left. How had she gotten herself and her family in so deep so quickly?

Pre-Mini, the Institute didn't need much capital, just enough for salaries for Margaret and Lee, rent, and typical office expenses. Sure, the video had cost, but almost immediately it had paid back. So fast that Margaret wanted Johanna to take a salary, but she had opted to wait so that they could invest in the Mini. Now she was pouring cash in, not taking it out. Maybe Dan would say get out, although he wasn't a quitter. She had the children to support. She had legal fees which were huge and could potentially keep growing. What if they lost? Was this the first time she had even allowed herself to voice this fear? What if a court 2000 miles away in New York said the Institute had to pay damages? She was the Institute. The money would have to come from her. Money that should be for their boys.

Two thousand miles seemed so far, but the law could reach here and menace her family. It could invade this tennis club for Anglos with its lush grass lawn in grass-less Santa Fe and demand restitution. She closed her eyes and fought the Looney-Tunes image of the long arm of the law with its huge blunt white-gloved hand stretching up the club drive trying to grab her ankle. She would, she decided, sit here for a moment and let these big willow trees protect her from the blistering Southwest sun. She'd calm herself among the rose bushes and peonies ringing the groomed courts.

Sitting alone with her worries, she wondered how much time had passed. She needed to get back to work. Time to stop thinking about her problems for now. The shade had turned to chill and her feet felt cold. Her body felt tight. She put on her sneakers, found her way to the convertible and put the top up. She didn't feel any closer to an answer, but knew that as always, she would go back to the office and face the music. Hadn't it been just the other day that they had all been a solid team?

"How was your game?" Lee asked.

"I actually beat Kathleen 6-3 in two sets."

"Cool. I guess the tennis clinic you took last month helped your serve."

"Maybe. Or else when I see the ball, I visualize it as Gross's head, and slam it across the net. Any calls?"

"Two for you. Liz Cody from *Shaping* Magazine wants to do an article on five Pilates exercises that will trim thighs fast. A sort of "*Thin Thighs in 30 Days*" deal. Then, a Dr. Paul Blanik, a PhD exercise physiologist from Atlanta, wants to see our research comparing the intensity of abdominal contractions from the Pilates Roll-Up with the Crunch," said Lee, rolling her eyes to the skylight.

"So, on the one hand we are Fat Central and on the other we are supposed to be conducting double blind studies. Which one do I call first?"

"Not Mr. PhD. He doesn't believe Pilates can do anything except get undeserved publicity. Which makes the public find fault with the real fitness experts, like him, who aren't giving them the body of their dreams," Lee said sarcastically.

"The PhDs, the exercise physiologists, all the degreed fellows are now going after us," said Johanna. "Maybe we should take this as a compliment. They ignored us until now. This means we are getting to them. Of course, we also have no studies, no proof. Just results. Just better bodies. But at this point, the more these experts disparage us, the more the public wants to give us a try."

"But they're not going to give up their crunches."

"What a business we're in. Can you believe that an exercise with a name like crunch—which you know that Webster's defines as crush—has become the fitness world's signature move. We live with gravity pushing us down and they get millions to make this worse by doing 50 plus reps of this bio-mechanically poor contraction when we should be lengthening our bodies. Improving our alignment. But their PhDs have studies that show it supposedly works. Can't people feel that they are just stressing their hip flexors and tensing their neck? Most of a crunch is just momentum, not abdominals working. Why don't they feel what their bodies are telling them rather than read these dumb studies?"

"Remember what PhD stands for?" Lee asked.

"I have heard this one. I just can't remember..."

"I'll make it easy. B.S. stands for—"

"I know, it is on my diploma."

" Ok. Well then M.S. is 'more of the same'. And PhD is 'piled higher and deeper'."

Johanna laughed out loud for the first time that day, maybe for the first time in a week. She started and didn't stop. Almost choked, but she still felt so much better.

"You know that I am the only one in this town who would laugh at that joke. Anything, everything that hasn't even been invented yet, offends everyone here in Wimpville, USA. This is truly the capital of New Age phoniness."

"I bet I couldn't tell it in Boston now either. Politically correct is the preferred mode everywhere. You might as well just stay here in Santa Fe where it began. Maybe it will end here first."

"No chance. Politically correct goes with our need for experts. We are living in the time of experts. If everything requires an expert than you don't have to take responsibility for anything outside of your expert-ise. You need to hire an expert to organize your closet. Guys on cooking shows make it appear that slicing an onion is as difficult as open-heart surgery. A friend of mine's kid started planning for graduate school the day after she got accepted to Yale. The public is convinced that you need an advanced degree to get a job process-ing purchase orders."

"That kid will need to work until she's ninety just to pay back the cost of her education," Lee predicted.

"True. But she'll keep adding initials to her name. Graduate school is where we warehouse our young adults since we don't have jobs for them."

"Hey. We're doing our part. Every Pilates teacher has a job the day after they are certified."

"For that, we have to thank the media. I think we are up to 50 major stories, and I'm not counting anything less than a page. The *Health Industry* article was four pages of raves. The fitness industry still can't believe that this wimpy exercise method has caught the fancy of the press. For sure, they thought it would fade in a couple of years. Now they are afraid it's got legs," Johanna agreed.

"It's got legs. And bodies, too. Pilates bodies."

14

NEW PEOPLE

"There's a renewed focus on wellness in the nineties and Pilates fits into that."

—USA Today, 1996

Johanna admitted, but only to herself, that her much admired steel gut wasn't holding up as well as Margaret believed. She felt nervous and tired. Was it because she did nothing other than sit and talk and figure? When had she last played tennis? Or moved some muscles on the Reformer? She knew that inactivity could spiral into neck pain, weight gain and more. No surprises here, just an all-too-familiar pattern that she had to short circuit. She had heard it so many times before, but thought that it could never happen to her. Hadn't she practically lied to Meredith about her frame of mind the last time they talked? Sitting on the sofa that evening alone, Johanna felt immobilized just as she had after Dan died. Not that it mattered. She had no place to go anyway.

She did have a few acquaintances, however. One of them, Sondra Brummel, was a ceramist who eked out a

living in her studio and spent her free time as an art guide
for trust funders, rich Texans and under-employed
Europeans.   People like Guy de Blanque, son of French
nobility, whose family name conferred on   him a minor
celebrity status. Johanna had heard about his looks, charm,
and parties—not that she'd been invited any place since
Dan died. She had one track: home, work, back. Sensibly,
she had regularly shifted her seat on the Italian couch, there-
by avoiding a permanent indentation of her ass.

Then one day, an unexpected telephone message.
Like the refrain of her favorite song, "What a difference a
day makes. Twenty four little hours." Sondra, a regular on
the party circuit, surprised her with an invitation, a chance
to change her routine.   At first hesitant, looking for an
excuse not to go, she began by saying no thanks, but
abruptly changed her mind and accepted. Sondra assured
her they would not be the token unattached women.
Johanna suspected that, behind the invite, might be her
need for transport to the party in something other than her
battered old, unreliable Datsun pick-up. Sondra promised
her that she had a return ride so Johanna would be free to
leave when she wanted.

A week later, as they turned left off Paseo de Peralta
at the pink Scottish Rite Temple, the directional marker for
getting onto Bishop's Lodge Road, Johanna realized that she
was actually feeling better. Lighter. Almost happy.   Out of

the house and off her couch, cruising the chamiso-lined road with Sondra was almost medicinal. As they made their way out of town and drove past Bishop's Lodge Resort, the air turned several degrees cooler. Sondra reached into the back of the convertible and grabbed her sweater just as Johanna took the sharp turn into Tesuque village.

"This is great! Things change here so fast! In New York we'd have to drive three hours to the barn for a real change of scenery."

"It's the water that makes the difference. The river, which no one can ever see, runs just behind those Russian Olive and Cottonwood trees on your right. Wait until you see the Tamarisk and fruit orchards at Guy's estate."

"I can't tell a maple from a pine. What's foliage? I thought I was going to need help with the guest names. Now you're telling me I need a trail map?"

They made their way past a roadside market and a small adobe post office.

"Just there on your right. See the wooded gate post?"

"This is typical New Mexican understatement. I was expecting something more grand after the things you've said," Johanna exclaimed, turning into a narrow dirt driveway.

"Just wait!" said Sondra.

As she drove into the compound, an orchard's formal lines of fruit trees spread out along the one side of the road followed by several low adobe casitas, obviously staff housing. Beyond the other side of the road, an expanse of garden with steel kinetic sculptures, Jesus Morales stone totems and old wagon wheels led up to the main house, an impressive territorial-style hacienda. In the parking area, she counted about thirty cars. The usual SUVs and a few ultra -chic vintage pick-up trucks. Also several ostentatious Jags and Mercedes, unusual in this pretend Wild West playground. Checking her hair in the mirror, she smoothed down her tight Alaia black sheath that nicely showcased her Pilates body.

She reached for her signature fragrance, Chanel No. 5.

Sondra gave her a curious look.

"Why bother? Can't you smell the flowers?"

"What's wrong? Don't tell me this is a fragrance-free event! I thought you said he was French!"

"I don't know what you think is in that bottle. The place is already dripping with real jasmine, rose, citron, and lavender . You look gorgeous, anyway," Sondra said. "Don't worry. You'll be the chicest one here."

They reached the main entrance from long path leading to the typical portico. A butler type opened the huge Spanish door to the sounds of understated live music.

Out on the terrazzo patio, a jazz quartet played something by Miles Davis for the mostly over-forty crowd whose animated chatter was obviously lubricated from the plentiful liquid refreshments.

Johanna turned to Sondra and whispered, "Merci." She smiled and squeezed her arm. "De Nada."

It did seem promising. French conversation and the pungent aroma of Gitane cigarettes were in the air. Accepting a glass of French champagne from a gorgeous waiter in white shirt and black tie, she took a long sip. She looked at Sondra with a 'where's the host?' question.

"You know what's funny?" Sondra said. "He's hardly ever here, maybe a month or two out of the year. It's his parents' place, one of several."

She glanced around trying to discern which man was Guy. "Is he here?" she asked.

Sondra laughed. "I wouldn't put it past him to throw a party and then not show up. Didn't Gatsby do that?"

Just then, she noticed a dark haired man on the other side of the pool in a black linen jacket and well cut jeans glancing at her. He had a sexy, European look that made American men appear dry-cleaned by comparison. He held a martini glass to his lips while appearing to listen intently to an elderly lady loaded down with many strands of turquoise, interspersed with large amber rocks.

"You spotted him," Sondra said. "That's Ariana Finch, the potter that he's speaking with."

She nodded. He was gorgeous. Wavy hair brushed rakishly back, a tan that set off the slightly unshaven jaw, and an easy but nuanced smile. She could tell from his expression that he was flattering the potter, but his eyes kept dancing over to her.

"Be warned," a woman's voice announced. "He's as dangerous as he looks."

Peeling her eyes from Guy, she spotted a sleek blonde sidling up to Sondra.

"Buffy," Sondra said. "I heard you were back. Meet Johanna Breyers."

Buffy was the only other woman at the party sleeker than Johanna.

"It's a pleasure," Buffy said as they shook hands.

She was model-thin, deeply toned, and wore layers of silver chains at both the wrist and neckline. But the most startling thing about Buffy was her hair. Pure angelic white blonde. And all natural, too. Probably everyone thought it was lightened, but after years in the salon business, Johanna could spot a convertible top at ten feet. Even figure out the formulation and the cost of its upkeep. Buffy's color was the real thing. 'Your hair is your most important fashion accessory' had been the advertising tag line when she worked in the salon business. Buffy's hair was a genuine asset.

"You're not from here?"

"No. Far from here."

There were a few extra syllables squeezed into the 'o' sound and Johanna tried to place the accent. "Australia?" she said.

"South Africa," Buffy said.

"Johanna's from New Yawk," Sondra said, affecting the clichéd accent. "But we've claimed her as one of our own." She winked. "Buffy is a recent recruit too. She left LA, its smog and freeways, and found our paradise."

Buffy placed her Gucci handbag on an adjacent table and took a glass of white wine from the eager waiter. Facing Johanna with a dazzling smile that showed her super white, obviously bleached teeth, she asked, "When did you arrive in Santa Fe?"

"Six years ago, but right now I am hardly enjoying paradise. Since I started working again, it seems no different from where I left. I spend 10 hours a day in a small office that could be anywhere."

"Let me guess. It's a start-up venture or you are a lawyer."

"Maybe I should get my law degree. I probably could pass the bar, and I've never been to law school. But the answer is yes. I started the Pilates Institute three years ago. Have you heard of Pilates?"

"Yes, brillant! Just read the article in *Lear's* magazine about what your Institute is doing to spread the word. In LA, a friend was going to the Flacher studio and told me about it just at the time that I was sideswiped by a huge, gas-guzzling SUV during my morning run. Since then, the only exercise I do is what the physical therapist gives me. But I want to try it now that I have her permission to start moving again."

"You know Pilates is not aerobic, right?"

"I've been a runner all my life and never had any knee or hip problems, but this freak accident may be a sign."

"Signs...you'll fit in here. I am superstitious too, though no one calls it that in this New Age place. It has had an upgrade. They refer to it here as 'psychic energy'."

"Hmmm." Buffy nodded slowly, then parted her lips into a wide smile that was both knowing and hungry. "My psychic energy is directed toward marketing. Mostly infomercials."

Johanna took a sip of champagne and nodded. Buffy intrigued her. She wasn't beautiful, but striking despite her overly large features. Magnetic was the word for her. Johanna actually felt her breath quicken from this attraction. What did they call this in 'New Age' speak? It's her aura. And it was powerful.

Over her shoulder, Johanna watched as Guy extracted himself from the older woman with a graceful squeeze of her arm, then glided toward them. His left hand stuffed casually in the front pocket of his jeans, he nodded and said hello to a few of his guests on the way.

"Uh oh," Buffy said. "Here comes trouble."

Guy was just close enough to hear her remark. He

smiled, took Buffy's hand and kissed it while keeping his eyes ahead toward Johanna. "Don't believe a word this woman says. She's a notorious exaggerator." His French accent pulled Johanna into something close to longing. Between the magnetism of Buffy and that of Guy, she felt a rush. Maybe, just maybe, her very dry, very lonely life would recede into history.

Buffy smiled ironically then extracted her hand from Guy's. "I suppose you want me to introduce you to my friend Johanna here."

Guy bowed graciously. "I shall have you removed from the premises if you don't." He faced her again. "Johanna?"

Johanna extended her hand. "Johanna Breyers. "You have a lovely home."

He took her hand and kissed it. "It's not mine. It's my parents. But who's keeping track. Now, Johanna, why haven't we met before? Tell me you've only moved to Santa Fe this very instant."

Buffy shook her head in mock ridicule. "Guy, you're slipping. You've let this gorgeous woman reside in Santa Fe for..." she turned. "Tell Guy how long you've been here."

"Six years," Johanna said.

Guy shook his head while flashing a dazzling smile. "I shall fire my spies at once."

Buffy, pleased that she had shown Guy that he wasn't always right, decided that she would do better with some of the other guests and seeing a chubby man in too tight jeans on the other side of the pool remarked, "I have to mingle now," she said. "Johanna, if you need rescuing from this impossible womanizer, sends up a flare or something."

She took her wine glass and sashayed on her three-inch heels across the deck.

Guy stood close to Johanna and watched Buffy leave. "It's true," he said.

"What? That you're a womanizer?"

He shook his head while talking. "About Buffy," he said. "She's devious. You should not trust her."

She turned to face him. "And why should I trust you?"

He laid a knee-weakening smile on her. "You shouldn't. I have only the worst intentions."

A waiter walked by with an empty tray and Guy beckoned him over. In the distance, Buffy spoke with several guests while winking at Johanna.

After a brief discussion in hushed tones, Guy sent the waiter on his way. "Watch this," he said. "I intend to clear this party out in less than an hour."

"How?"

He laughed. "I've told the staff to stop serving. When the liquor is no more, they'll be in their cars in no time. Some will go directly to their AA meeting. There's one every hour in this town."

"Are you not enjoying your own party?"

He took a sip of his Martini and glanced out at his min-gling guests. "I'll enjoy it more once we winnow the crowd a bit."

The exodus followed as he had described it. Guy had obviously used this ploy before. As the waiters removed the last of the wine, tequila, and other spirits, the guests snapped at them as if it were their last chance to drink before a long journey. No reinforcements followed and within the hour, the crowd began to thin. Guy remained with Johanna by the edge of his pool deck as guests paraded by to offer thanks. He introduced her to everyone as if she were his girlfriend. Buffy came by, kissed him on both cheeks, and warned him to be nice.

"It was lovely meeting you, Johanna," she said. "We should talk some time. Are you in the book?"

"I am," she said. "Call me."

15

GUY

"Until his death in 1967, Joseph Pilates... taught a group of grateful professional dancers his own quirky conditioning rehabilitation...30 years later, fitness enthusiasts would clamor for the Pilates workout as the ticket to a long, lean dancer's body."
—The New York Times, 1996

Guy winnowed the crowd all right. By 9:30 he'd winnowed it all the way down to the clean-up staff and Johanna. It all happened so smoothly and so naturally, she barely had time to react. He had commanded a staff of 10 so he'd be free to seduce her and, other than an introductory kiss, had barely touched her.

"Now then," he said. He went to the emptied bar and retrieved a bottle of Moet from a cabinet underneath along with two champagne glasses. "I think the moon is over..." He glanced around the corner of the pool house and pointed. "There. Come." He stuck his elbow out and she held onto it.

"I've already had two glasses," she said. "And I have to drive home tonight."

He laughed as he led her from across the pool deck to a small balcony on the pool house. "Mais oui. You must drive home," he said.

Out on the balcony, they watched the last cars make their way down the winding drive as the surrounding hills glistened in silvery moonlight.

Guy leaned against the balcony and fingered the tie on Johanna's dress. "Tell me about Pilates," he said. "I understand it does wonderful things to the body. Perhaps you could show me."

She removed his hand from her dress. "I'd be happy to arrange a private lesson with my partner, Margaret, who is a wonderful teacher."

Guy inched a bit closer to her. "I don't know this Margaret. Is she as beautiful as you?"

Johanna shook her head.

He shrugged. "This is a problem then. I am only capable to learn things from beautiful women."

"So I hear."

When he smiled his white teeth shone against his

tanned skin and the corners of his eyes wrinkled. "Does what you've heard about me bother you?"

Talk about a loaded question. But when she paused to think about it, it didn't.

"No," she said.

Guy stepped closer and placed his hand on the small of her back. Their torsos were almost but not quite touching and she could feel the heat radiating between them despite the cooling night air. A mischievous breeze fluttered the hem of her dress and her skin felt electric.

Guy smiled, but said nothing. He didn't have to. What was about to happen was obvious, as obvious as the ivory moon rising over the Tesuque hills.

Johanna and Guy spent the next morning enjoying each other's company. They wandered a path on the estate that led to the river, then on to the stables. Lunch in the garden overlooking the Tesuque valley stirred some old memories of a family vacation in the South of France. Later, relaxing by the pool, the surroundings and the sun, ushered her back to the fragrances, the flowers, the warm French air and the long siestas. Alone with her thoughts, Guy interrupted her reverie.

"Cherie, shall we take a swim ? Look in the cabana

if you need pool things."

Perfect, Johanna thought. Let's see who else swims here.   As expected, here were too many size 2 French designer labels to ignore. Bikinis so small they seemed beside the point. Why bother? Johanna undressed, found a bottle of   Clarins suntan lotion, applied it to parts rarely exposed to sunlight, and then   made her way back to the pool. "Nice sunglasses," Guy playfully commented.

It was apparent that living well was Guy's natural state. He approached life with gusto and sprezzatura: generous, relaxed, without an uptight bone in his body. Accustomed to wealth, he never spoke about the cost of anything.

Johanna, ever hopeful, but not totally naïve had no illusions about whether there were others, yesterday or even later this evening. He had taken two calls already that day and had spoken a bit too hushed during the conversation in the garden in particular. Since Dan had died she had been alone and wasn't sure what she was up for herself. For now, this was all she needed.

Driving away down his winding road early that evening as the summer clouds began to tumble in, she felt loose, happy. Some part of her that she'd ignored had been awakened. She felt re-connected to the happier times she'd known before these last wrenching years. Saner. She had no doubt there was a lot of competition for his company, but maybe right now, they were elsewhere, even abroad.

The sky darkened and a gentle shower welcomed her home. She ran through the warm rain with a lightness she hadn't felt in years. Inside the message light on her answering machine was blinking red. Hoping it was a goodnight kiss from Guy, she pressed the play button.

"Hi Johanna. It's Buffy here. It was really wonderful meeting you. I hope Guy was a gentleman. Though I doubt very much that he was. Maybe we could have lunch some time soon. I really want to know more about Pilates. Give me a call when you have a chance. 983-8867 Byee."

There was something soothing about the familiarity in Buffy's tone of voice. An unexpected intimacy. Her sophisticated yet warm manner reminded Johanna of New York friends she missed. So different from her Santa Fe acquaintances—predictable, serious, earnest, over-educated, well meaning, and also boring. Not like Buffy. And certainly not like Guy.

She thought about Buffy and just knew that they would become involved on some level soon. She would ask her opinion about marketing Pilates. She needed to find out more about infomercials, Buffy's specialty, and if they might work for Pilates. Impulsively, she turned on the TV and found a cable channel that ran them exclusively. An attractive blonde, Jennifer, was demo-ing a pancake gadget that could turn out dozens of perfectly shaped circles without any mess or waste. Just what America needed. Next up was a program that she did know—who didn't—Suzanne Somers' and her Thigh Master. As the blonde bombshell parted and closed her lithe thighs around the contraption, Johanna's gears began to turn, and then turn faster. She had to will herself not to get up and pace, to stay glued to the Thigh Master. It was nothing more than Joe Pilates' Magic Circle. He'd invented it decades ago. Maybe Somers had seen one at the Flacher studio in Beverly Hills. Here she was on TV, selling Pilates and she *never* mentioned the P word! Brilliant.....

16

BUFFY

"Credit Pilates' growing popularity to celebrities such as Vanessa Williams, Jodie Foster, Courtney Cox, Demi Moore and Jane Seymour who are fans."
—The Baltimore Sun, 1997

Johanna returned Buffy's call the next day. They chatted briefly, just long enough to set up a lunch. Thursday at Coyote Cantina was as soon as they could both make it. The Cantina, the casual rooftop addition to Mark Miller's famous Coyote Café, served his unique blend of Old Mexico cuisine with today's lighter style, and best of all, the tables were outside, shaded by an awning. For Johanna, everything tasted better with fresh air.

"Tell me about Pilates," Buffy asked right after the waiter had left with their order.

"Translation, what Pilates will do for you. It always comes down to the personal. It's very subjective. The history and the theory are just background noise. So for starters, you will regain range of motion in your hip that you lost

161

from the accident. Once that's fixed, we'll be on to the important stuff like shaping and toning, not that you are needy in that department. You obviously got into the right body line at birth. You can't compare Pilates with aerobics. There's no endorphin rush like the one you get from running."

"Can't start running yet anyway, so I'd love to try it. How many times a week do you do Pilates?"

"Why is that the second question everyone asks me? When I tell them twice a week, they are amazed."

"You can get that body in two hours a week?"

"As I said, choose your parents very carefully. Pilates can tone and lengthen, but nothing changes your bones. Still, I think it's the best exercise you can learn. I said learn, not just do. It is quality exercise. Not 'less is more' as we know that expression. But Pilates teaches how to move correctly, and once you 'get it' every movement conditions the whole body."

"I'm envious. It must be such a pleasure to work for something you believe in."

"Frankly I'm having trouble keeping the faith right now. Legal problems with the trademark, legal problems with the prototype. Problems cost. Next we'll have more than just mundane money problems. If growing a business is akin to regular growing pains, then my growth spurts are hurting a lot."

"Start-ups always have problems. Plus you are, in effect, birthing an industry. I have heard about the trademark dispute. Some physical therapist in New York bought it secondhand from the previous owner who had gone broke and didn't protect it. An unprotected trademark is like unprotected sex. It is a big mistake."

"Mistakes fuel lawyers and legal bills.   The legal hourly rate is three times what a PT can charge. I am counting on this spread to work in my favor. He's got to be in pain."

"He's probably suffering so much he needs a PT to work on him. So what's this prototype for?"

"It's a fold-up version of the Reformer. When you come for your lesson I'll show it to you."

"I am so ready to be reformed. Just tell me when."

During the subsequent months, Johanna juggled questions from trademark lawyers, their own and those of her tormentors, their patent lawyer, Randall Whitethorpe, and

their   recently retained consulting engineer. More important, and much more pleasurable, were the calls she fielded
from Institute members, fitness writers, and aerobic trainers deciding whether to switch. It seemed as if the phone was
attached to her ear and the chair to her ass. The time when
she could enjoy the perfect New Mexican climate or having
an entire Pilates studio down a flight of stairs was receding
into a distant place. Margaret was teaching. Lee was mailing videos and membership information, and Johanna was
battling, tilting at the occasional windmill. From time to
time, Johanna talked to Buffy about the Institute and
Buffy's growing infatuation with the Pilates Method.

"I'm totally hooked," Buffy called out from the
Reformer one late afternoon to Johanna as she descended
the stairs. Johanna walked over and sat on the window
ledge. Buffy looked great and now moved with what
Johanna assumed was her former ease.

"I'm glad that you are lovin' it because every time I
lie down on that comfortable upholstered carriage all I can
think about are manufacturing costs, product liability
insurance policies, and UPS shipping requirements. Or else
I just want to close my eyes and sleep for a very long time,"
Johanna confessed.

"Johanna, anyone else but you would be dead
already from trying to do this by yourself. Manufacturing,

marketing, distribution, inventory, returns, this is a very capital intensive and treacherous business. You really need to partner," Buffy said.

"You mean an investor who will fund this machine?" said Johanna.

"Yes, that's the best way to go so that you control the marketing. If you can't get that, a licensee deal is the second choice. As you found out, you can't manufacture it here. Lagune's prices were way too high. You need help to find a manufacturing partner with Asian factories. You are in a defensive mode because you are battling the trademark lawsuit. You can't expect yourself to easily switch to a selling mode. But I can sell this opportunity, source out any possible deals. I have the time, and I love Pilates."

"Buffy, trust me, you will talk yourself sick. First they pretend that they have never heard of Pilates. Then you show them 200 plus articles that have been published in the past 3 years and they say they "don't get it." Then you explain to them that there are hundreds of exercises that one can do on this machine that looks like an ironing board or a medieval torture device—take your pick—and then they get defensive since they are still doing dumb crunches or whatever," Johanna ranted. "This is not like talking to an investor or a marketing person about some new computer technology or a fuel-efficient car. It's personal.

It ends up being about their own fat thighs and their carbs. Everyone in this damn country is neurotic about his or her own body."

"But business people are looking for the next great body solution. It's the biggest market, excuse the pun," said Buffy.

"Right. It's big. Huge. Hugely crazy. The fitness revolution is 25 years old which is ancient in diet years. People are invested in whatever they have done or not done. When women ask me how I stay thin I used to think that they really wanted to know my regimen. But they don't. They want   confirmation of their choices or their excuses. So they don't lose weight because they think that if you don't exercise for an hour every day and eat only fruits and vegetables and drink tons of Perrier or Evian water or whatever tops the water purity charts this week, you don't deserve to have a better body.   It's so sick I can't stand it any more. Fifty percent of the adult population is fat.   The media is all over diets and exercise. Magazines that have nothing to do with health and beauty run exercise and diet articles. I bet *Popular Mechanics* has run an article on bigger biceps: *Which Works Faster, a Sledge Hammer or a Tapping Hammer?*"

"I am not going to tell you to take a deep breath and try to calm your inner self because you are too far gone for this kind of counsel," Buffy advised. "You need to get away from this studio pronto. I am changing my clothes and then we are leaving and going to the Pink for a drink. Make that several. Then dinner. Afterwards you will call Guy and tell him to get over to your house since you will not be in driving condition. You need some French style relaxation. Stop worrying. I have a plan on how to get this adorable mini machine made," said Buffy.

And Buffy did indeed have a plan that included her as their agent and a partner in whatever deal she could find. But first they had to spend more money and time. For example, Buffy needed a video showing an exercise routine—better several—on the Mini Reformer. How else to convince prospects that this little slider is more than just a machine for leg exercises? That this machine could replace an entire gym. Margaret reluctantly agreed to direct the videos even though she really wanted to drop the entire project and focus on the legal battle. She thought they were spread too thin, but Johanna couldn't stop herself. From the first lunch with Buffy, Johanna knew that she would follow wherever Buffy led her. Buffy made her feel that the two of them already were partners. Johanna didn't need convincing because she felt they already had a shared history, and that something new, like the Pilates Mini-Reformer, was a continuation, another phase of their existing partnership.

17

THE TRADEMARK

"Joseph Pilates, the late inventor of the popular exercise system... never sought a trademark. Instead...he bequeathed it to the world, through a core group of followers who "went out and spread the word".
—The New York Times Magazine, 1997

Johanna was in the office pawing through a huge pile of discovery documents that their lawyer had sent over when Margaret phoned her to say she wouldn't be coming in. There was deadness in her voice, a dislocation from her words. Before Johanna could probe further, the other line rang and Lee answered it.

"Yes, Buffy, hang on," Lee said as she turned toward Johanna.

"Margaret," Johanna said. "Buffy's calling. I'll phone you later."

"Right."

Buffy was in New York 'on business and shopping' in her own words. "Oh God," Buffy swooned. "I miss

New York. It's gorgeous. Crisp and yet sunny. Everyone's out in Soho. You won't even believe the skirt I just bought at Ralph Lauren. Big sale. Jam-packed. I almost came to blows with a member of Generation X, but Johanna, I'm telling you it was worth it. Just above the knee, peacock blue, one of a kind. Amazing. I'm on my way to Otto Tootsie for shoes right now."

Buffy's words made Johanna hungry, but not for shoes. She ran a list through her mind of her favorite eating haunts.

"Tell me you've had a corned beef on rye at Carnegie Deli," she said. "Don't spare the delicious details."

Buffy laughed hysterically. Johanna could hear the jumble of voices from the sidewalk crush all around her. "Are you kidding me? I'd be on the Stairmaster for the rest of my life after that. No. I went to Jerry's for an omelette and tonight I'm meeting friends at Odeon."

Closing her eyes, she let Buffy's words transport her back home. You don't really leave New York. It won't let you. Once you feel at home there, every place else just seems less.

"Johanna," she said. "Have you done the Seaweed Wrap at Aveda?"

She hadn't, but she wasn't in the mood to hear about it either.

"You've got to try their wrap," Buffy rhapsodized. "I feel two sizes smaller."

As Buffy described her two days sampling the culinary and fashion offerings of Manhattan, Johanna's mind could only focus on why she was stuck in Santa Fe trying to manufacturer a machine that was sinking them deeper into problems.

"Oh, and I met with Steve Gross yesterday. Jeeze, Johanna, you never told me he's fat. I can't believe he's a physical therapist."

She spun her chair from the window so quickly she almost fell out of it. "Steve Gross?" She said. "Why are you meeting with Steve Gross?"

"Hold on," Buffy said. Her muffled voice asked a street vendor the price on a bracelet. "What?" She said. "I'm sorry, Johanna. It's so noisy here."

"Steve Gross," she said, her volume rising. "You met with Gross?"

From the background noise Johanna inferred she'd

left the bracelet behind. "Look, Johanna," Buffy assured. "Don't worry about Steve Gross. Everything's under control. That's what I was calling about. They want to do the deal. You have a manufacturing and marketing partner willing to do what you need. Isn't that great?"

"That is great," she said. "That's excellent news. But—"

"Ooh, ooh," squealed Buffy. "Excuse me, how much is that bag? No, that one. Is that Gucci? Probably a knock off, right? Ooh, what about that one?"

"Buffy," Johanna said, demanding attention.

"Sorry, Johanna," the exuberant shopper apologized. "I can't stop myself. I need an intervention here! Anyway, where were we? Oh yeah. They're in. They want to do this. All we have to do is settle the Trademark thing with Steve Gross."

"Settle?" Johanna's voice rose on the second syllable. "What do you mean settle?"

"You will not believe how crowded it is here. Every shop is having sales. Otto Tootsie is jam-packed and I really need shoes. What do you think of wedge heels? I'm not sure. They're a little heavy."

"Buffy," she said more than firmly "What do you mean by settle?"

Johanna heard the squeak of a door opening then the thump thump of rap music and the crush of hungry female fashonistas.

"Well the thing is," Buffy said over the noise. "We have to sell this as a Pilates machine. So we need Steve and Roberta on board. You know for the name. So you guys are going to have to kiss and make up. But don't worry. Steve's not that bad. It's not like you'll have to deal with him directly or anything."

"Buffy," she said. "Steve and Roberta are suing me. Remember?"

"No, no," Buffy soothed. "They're willing to settle. Don't worry about it. I have everything under control."

Johanna stood up from her chair and started pacing in the tiny office. Lee watched her pacing out of the corner of her eye as she typed at her Mac.

"Are you telling me," she said, "that they're going to drop the lawsuit?"

"Exactly," she said.

Johanna stopped pacing and focused on a calendar on the opposite wall. Lee had written in something for next week. Upon closer inspection she could make out Lee's handwriting. 'Margaret's birthday.'

"In exchange for what?" she continued.

"Oh my god," she said. "Thirty bucks? Are you kidding me? I'll take two pairs. Johanna, get on a plane and get down here right now. I am not kidding."

The shoe chat, which Buffy was using to detract from the issues, raised Johanna's blood pressure. But she had to know what was going on. "Buffy," she demanded.

"What are the terms?"

"The terms?" she said. "Oh yeah, all you have to do is change the name of your Institute. Drop Pilates."

Johanna dropped back into her chair.

"They want us to change the name of the Institute?" Johanna was incredulous.

"Who?" Buffy said. "Steve and Roberta? Yeah. That's it. Do that and we've got this deal in the bag."

"Buffy," she carefully explained. "I still believe that the trademark will not hold up. This is not just radical, it is a complete capitulation."

"Who cares about the trademark?" Buffy airily told her. "It's just a word. Look, the manufacturer, Body Machines, needs both your patent and Steve's trademark so we can all get going. Let's Make a Deal, Wheel of Fortune, The Price Is Right! Get on the band-wagon, girlfriend!"

"Okay, okay," Johanna muttered.

"Okay? Way more than okay," Buffy practically shouted, "You win. Because at the end of the day, it's your machine we're selling, not theirs. What do Steve and Roberta have to sell? They are small time. We're gonna make millions on this thing."

She heard a loud click and Buffy's voice swearing in the background.

"Sorry," she said. "I just dropped the phone. Listen, can I call you back? I've got to fish out my credit card. So, are we good to go?"

Johanna opened her mouth to speak, but quite possibly for the first time ever, no words came out.

"I'll call you back," Buffy said. "Buh-bye."

Johanna returned the phone to its cradle and stared blankly for a few seconds.

Lee stopped typing and faced her. "What was that all about? Oh, Margaret called back to say she's sick and we should cancel her clients for tomorrow."

"She can't be sick. Tell her I'm on my way over." Johanna said.

"Johanna, you may be many things to many people, but a faith healer you ain't. Bring me your tired, your weary, your poor. Nope, Johanna, the shoe doesn't seem to fit."

"If I hear one more fucking word about shoes I am going to really lose it."

Johanna took a breath and tried to calm herself. Lee was right, she wasn't exactly Ms. Understanding when it came to the subject of illness, probably because she was never sick. But she had to talk to Margaret. She needed her reaction to Buffy's proposal. No, not just her reaction. Margaret's careful and thorough assessment of where the Institute and they themselves stood. The reasons for her coldness. Her wavering commitment. The vacuum growing between them could no longer go unspoken. As for

Margaret being sick, Johanna wasn't feeling great either. There was an ongoing throbbing dullness in the back of her brain that she categorically assigned to Margaret's resistance. They had to talk.

"I'm going to run over and check in with Margaret. I'll take her some soup. Is that enough laying on of hands for you, Lee?"

Lee nodded. "Good. She likes that place on Marcy Street, Josie's. They've got a take-out window in the back of her store."

"I am on my way." Johanna grabbed her purse and left the office.

18

MARGARET

"The point of Pilates is to develop awareness of your body: how you move, stand, breathe—and yes even how you lie still. Even for the most sedentary people, Pilates promotes balance, flexibility and coordination—skills that help with everyday life."
—Spa Finder, 1997

Margaret lived in a casita she'd inherited from her parents, artists who had come to Santa Fe in the fifties when it was sleepy and hip, but before the buzz had turned it into a tourist mecca. The little house sat in the hills southeast of downtown several miles after the roads turned to dirt. Barking dogs welcomed Johanna into this Santa Fe non-neighborhood neighborhood. Sage and chamiso followed narrow dirt drives that turned off the road randomly. All poorly marked. It was impossible to decipher between roads, driveways or simple landings. No one wanted to be found at home, it seemed to Johanna, as she drove on another half mile. Not a visible house in sight. Johanna found the marker, a signpost that read Calle Garcia. She parked her Miata in the driveway and surveyed the property before stepping out of her car. She had learned early in her time in New Mexico this was a good way to let the dust settle and make friends with the animals. In just such a way she had met two

Vietnamese pigs, a llama, a goat, and numerous four and three-legged dogs. She waited and reflected on how lucky Margaret was to have this quiet haven.

With Josie's sopa de pollo in hand, Johanna knocked at the door and waited for what seemed a long time. Was Margaret asleep? Finally, she heard movement, but instead of opening the door, Margaret merely peered through a curtain in the living room window, obviously surprised, but not really happy, to see Johanna.

"Just a minute," she said. And she took that full minute before opening the door.

"Hello," Johanna said holding up the brown bag. "I hope it's still hot."

Margaret hesitated in the doorway as if searching for a reason to shoo her away. Then slowly opened the door and let her inside.

Margaret took the bag from Johanna and placed it on a cluttered counter that separated her small living room from an even smaller kitchen. "Would you like to sit down?"

Johanna moved a stack of dance magazines from a wing back chair and sat down. "Lee and I are getting worried about you. I understand that you need some space, but there is so much to talk about, things concerning Buffy. What's going on with you, Margaret?" Johanna detected a faint cedar smell and noticed smoke spiraling from an incense burner.

"I'm fine. What is going on in the office? What did Buffy want?"

"Are you sitting?"

Margaret laughed joylessly and slid onto a faded sofa. "What now?"

She told Margaret about the deal they'd have to make with Steve and Roberta in order to get the manufacturing partner. As she explained the offer, she found herself actually pitching the idea of the name change. Somewhere between the office and Margaret's house, she must have convinced herself of the inevitability of that decision, for here she was, making Buffy's case. She expected confrontation, but Margaret only sunk further, becoming one with the sofa.

"So what do you think?" Johanna asked after a long unanswered pause. "Do we dance with the devil to make this deal? Or do we fight Gross on the trademark? I need your take on this one."

Margaret pulled her long legs up into her chest and

clung to them. She took in a belabored breath. "The name has haunted our every step. It's the word we shouldn't have used. Change the name if you want. Do a deal with Gross or Buffy or whomever. Otherwise, we're just going to keep banging our heads against the wall. And getting sued. I no longer believe we know what we're doing. And I'm tired of listening to lawyers. I'm tired of the stress. I can't live with a lawsuit hanging over me. I don't want to deal with it any more," she said. "I can't deal with it any more. My body's rebelling."

"From the stress?" Johanna said. "You're sick from stress?"

She laughed sourly then narrowed her eyes at Johanna. "Yes," she said. "That's exactly it. I'm sick from stress."

"So take a few weeks off. We'll manage."

"Good!"

She was on her feet and into the kitchen. Across the counter, Johanna watched her turn the tap on and grip the tile sink with both hands.

"Margaret?"

The former dancer's shoulders rose and fell gently.

Johanna got up from the chair and rushed to her side.

"What is it?" she said. "What's wrong?"

Margaret pumped some antibacterial soap into her hands and rubbed them together under the stream. The smell of lemon wafted up. "Did you have your mammogram?" she asked Johanna. "Like we all promised?"

Johanna responded. "Yes I did."

"Did you get the results?"

"Of course," she said. "I'm fine. And you?"

Margaret turned off the tap and dried her hands on a dishrag hanging over a door handle under the sink. "Well I'm not," she said. "They found a lump."

"Oh, Margaret." Johanna reached for her hand but Margaret pushed it away and brushed past her out of the kitchen.

"And yes," she continued. "It is malignant. So as you can imagine, Johanna, I don't really give a damn about Buffy, or Steve, or Roberta, or the stupid trademark, or the patent, or the Mini-Reformer, or the name for that matter. I don't care about any of it. It wasn't worth it. None of it is worth it."

"Margaret, I'll handle the business. Let's talk about you. What about surgery or chemo?" she gently asked.

"Yes," she dryly responded. "Yes, to both. I'll start soon. Do what you want with the business. I'm not letting it stress me out any more. Do whatever you want. I've had enough. I've paid a high enough price already."

Margaret left the kitchen and walked down the hallway to her bedroom. Johanna thought she heard crying. For a moment Johanna considered going to comfort her, but it was clear that she didn't want that. She was too angry.

On the drive home Johanna replayed their conversation a half dozen times. Could Margaret possibly believe there was a correlation between their business concerns and her breast cancer? Was it medically possible? Johanna didn't know much about cancer. She didn't have an answer, but she knew that in the wake of such terrible news that she had to stop obsessing about the implications.

As soon as Johanna entered her house, she went right for the kitchen, opened the freezer and dug out some green chile chicken soup. Pacing around while it defrosted and then heated, she tried to figure out how she might have reduced the stress despite Eve's death, the lawsuit, her own aloneness. The hot soup warmed her, but she still felt chilled and shaky. Taking up her familiar seat on the Italian couch, she sat and thought and obsessed for what must have been hours. There was nothing she could do about Margaret's health. Women beat breast cancer every day. Margaret would, too. She got up from the couch to call Meredith. Probably Meredith knew about the latest treatments. She kept up with medical research, knew all the numbers, might be able to offer some nutritional advice. Meredith was also probably asleep. It was 11:30 on the East coast. Johanna put the phone down before the first ring. There was tomorrow.

Returning to the couch, she focused back to the one problem that she did have some measure of control over: the name of the Institute. No doubt about it. It was a defeat to change the name. But what if the trademark gang won just because all the law is on their side. The Institute would have to change their name anyway because they weren't going to teach Pilates the Roberta way. The name would come to represent her type of Pilates, and Johanna knew that alone would curtail its growth. It would hit its own glass ceiling. Maybe she'd been wrong about its potential anyway. Maybe they were just cursed. Or maybe the name was a curse. Kent Hemel's refusal to work with them. Nortrax's getting out of the contract, these weren't flukes. The fitness industry was dragging its feet on Pilates. The trademark issue had placed them in the untouchables caste. Pilates had become a threat, rather than an opportunity. Making millions by 'keeping it simple' had always been the mainstream fitness industry's mantra. Until 'go for the burn' and all its trappings became a saturated market who needed to confuse things with something new—even if it was better.

Johanna needed to make some decisions without Margaret for the time being, maybe longer. Tonight seemed as good a time as any. So it was clear: the Institute would go along with Buffy—and settle with Steve Gross and Roberta. Give up the Pilates name.

It was time to dance with the devil.

19

THE HINGE

"Pilates plans to pump itself up—by selling franchises. But franchisees might not wind up with exclusive use of name "Pilates". In franchise-offering papers, the company notes a trademark tiff in federal court in New York."

—Wall Street Journal, 1997

L ee faced the Mac and began typing different letter combinations trying to find a new name for the Institute. She brainstormed a hundred different options, but it was Johanna who finally produced the winner:

The BodyMind Institute.

To Johanna, that name represented the next level of Pilates, the convergence of the physical with the mental. Despite being strong-armed into the name change by the trademark gang, Johanna, ever aware of the silver lining, believed it was an opportunity to evolve Pilates even further.

Lee got to work right away on the new logo and letterhead and Johanna wrote the lead article for the next Forum introducing the name to their membership along with the slogan: *"Changing the name, not the Method."*

"We are not capitulating," Johanna reassured. "Pilates wasn't even the name Joe used. He called it contrology."

Margaret, now in chemotherapy, was rarely present in person, but even with her strength drained, her telephone calls were not in a passive voice.

"Why aren't we getting paid to create the videos and the workout charts and all the other materials? We do the work for no pay and then they sell our work for extra with the machine?" Margaret demanded.

"Unavoidable," Johanna said. "That's how these deals are done. No one gets paid up front. It is all on the come. You've heard that sweet expression."

"And Buffy?" Margaret said, her voice threatening. She had no time to drain her energy by concealing her distain. Her elegant manner was gone.

Johanna kept her eyes on her yellow legal pad. "Buffy put the deal together, Margaret. Again, that's how it is done."

"Business deals and business dealers are really, really low on the food chain. We kill ourselves for 4 years to create the Pilates industry, design the machine, get it patented, slug through 3 prototypes, produce all the materials and then they bless it by peeing on it with 'their' trade-mark. And why can't this big deal manufacturer pay for anything?"

"They are spending. There's the cost of the molds, and the raw materials, and the fabrication, and the inventory, and the returns. It's a very capital intensive business. That's why we all take risks. But once we start selling this machine it will return to us fast. The market is much bigger now. It won't be just for prospective teachers. Studios want them to sell to clients. Personal trainers can put them into their cars and take them to clients' houses to work them out. And some studios will add them to their studios for group Reformer classes. Who knows. Probably someday when we are retired it will sell at retail like everything else."

Margaret had had enough of this twisted logic. She closed off any further discussion with, "I don't know if I'll be around to see that happen."

Months passed and all the business deal types involved with the Mini Reformer seemed to be less and less available. In fact, they didn't seem to be on the same planet as the Institute. Buffy was always away. The manufacturer wouldn't take any more of their calls and referred all questions to Buffy who seemed to be in New York more than any shoe addict needed to be. They had turned in their videos and training tools and signed on the dotted line and now wanted to know where it stood. Finally, Buffy called from someplace unknown. Her voice was tight and strained.

"Sorry I have been unavailable, but I have been trying to work things out." Buffy said.

"Work out what? When do we see the Minis?"

"There's been a little problem. It seems that you don't really have a patent on that hinge. What you have is a design patent."

"What?! You knew that from the start. The hinge is covered in the design."

"Yes but the contract says that your hinge is specifically protected and it is not. You signed a contract saying that you had a patented hinge."

"Looks like it is time for our lawyer to respond to your accusations. You will hear from him today," said Johanna as she hung up the phone and immediately dialed Albuquerque.

Of course, it only got worse. The Mini Reformer was renamed the Pilates Body Former and the Institute got nothing. That meant more for Gross who re-negotiated his

his royalty and had it doubled since the Pilates name, according to his very smart lawyer, was what was needed to set this machine apart. To make it exclusive since anyone could just redesign it and get around the Institute patent. Design patents aren't useless, just not very protective. The manufacturing team felt that by generously rewarding Gross they were helping to defray the cost of his many infringement actions. After all, the manufacturer reasoned, without a strong patent, they needed the Pilates name even more.

"Hello?" a man's voice came from the studio downstairs.

"Guy?" Johanna said.

"May I come in?"

Johanna went downstairs and returned with the handsome Frenchman.

"I was in the neighborhood," he said. "I couldn't resist stopping in to see these machine of yours and...very strange indeed."

He had a quick look around the decidedly unglamorous office with its second-hand copier and stuttering printer.

"Oh," Johanna said. "You mean the Pilates machines."

He smiled generously revealing stunning white teeth.

"Would you like to go for some coffee?" she asked.

He shook his head. "I hope I'm not interrupting your work." He faced her and placed a hand delicately on her arm. "How is it with your mini machine?"

Lee looked at Johanna expectantly, and then she turned back to her Mac to give them some privacy.

"That good?" Guy said. "What did I tell you about Buffy? She looks after herself first and always."

Buffy was a topic that Lee avoided. Johanna didn't want to get into the subject either.

"No," Johanna said. "It's all going fine. These things take time to get established. We're just hitting some bumps, that's all. Isn't it lunchtime? Have you eaten?"

"No," Guy said. "I was hoping to take you away for a long lunch."

In the pregnant pause that followed, Lee doubted whether Johanna would return to the office after her "lunch" with Guy. And she didn't. Guy had been right about Buffy. Although Johanna had glossed over their problems, the problems just got worse. The Institute was too small to stand up to their former partners, now their adversaries, whose lawyers toyed with them at a distance. For the Institute, the Mini-Reformer debacle almost put them out of business. The humiliation was as painful as the unpaid royalties.

"I don't understand," Lee said. "We have a patent. How can they manufacture our machine and not pay us a royalty?"

"Lee," Johanna said. "Flashback to my meeting with Randall Whitethorpe. Did I or did I not ask him what kind of patent we needed?"

"I wasn't at that meeting," she reminded her.

"I know! But I told you about it. Didn't I tell you I specifically asked him whether we needed a design patent or a functional patent?"

It was all coming back to her. Margaret and Johanna had returned from that meeting in foul moods.

"Well, guess what? Design patents are essentially useless as protection. They are useful in patent lawsuits, however."

"What are you saying?"

"We sue and the bucks roll out of here and into some lawyers' accounts," Johanna explained.

"But surely we will win in court."

Johanna exhaled in frustration. "In court," she said. "Lawyers. More lawyers."

As the trademark gang gained in strength with the royalties from the Body Former, the validity of the mark looked more assured. Johanna's continued belief that it could be challenged isolated her even more. Her previous boast that she could easily pass the LSATs began to look like the joke was on her. The trademark gang positioned themselves to take over what everyone in the Pilates community had built. They assumed that the Institute would have enough sense to go out of business. Then they would really own Pilates—name, patents, certification, membership and all the future deals that would roll in once they were the only game. With Buffy's assistance, a TV deal with a home shopping channel was made and *voila,* the Mini-Reformer, or Body Former by Pilates, became hugely successful generating millions to pay for more lawyers to sue more Pilates teachers, even those not using the mark, just teaching on a Reformer.

The Institute was left with nothing. Unless, that is, you

you counted all the lawyers' fees incurred in their next lawsuit. This one for patent infringement which seemed their only chance for justice. Johanna, unaware that an average patent lawsuit requires a legal fund of about three million dollars, plunged ahead fueled only by her desperation and anger into a fight she had no chance of winning, only to waste hundreds of thousands and jeopardize her health just to arrive at that conclusion. Johanna had always taken for granted her perfect health. She used to say that no one would go to medical school if she were typical. She never got sick. Never even had a common cold, never missed a day of work. She had always downplayed the impact of stress. For the first time in her life, it began to take its toll on her body. She developed abdominal pains so severe she'd have to lie down in the office until they went away. She admitted that her immune system was finally acting like everyone else's.

"It is a good thing that you never completed that story you were writing for the Forum. The one you had titled, 'Pilates Power'," Johanna commented to Lee.

"Well that was two years ago when you still had your superwoman constitution." Lee recalled that day and the bizarre incident that had given her the story idea. Johanna had called the office and asked Lee to interrupt Margaret who was downstairs supervising certification students teaching their practice clients. Margaret came upstairs and Lee listened to her side of the conversation.

"Is it black?" Margaret said emphatically.

"But is it shiny?"

"It doesn't have to be as black as patent leather. If it is black and has a red dot, put it in a jar and bring it in now."

Margaret put down the phone and went back to supervising. About forty minutes later Johanna arrived at the Institute, started to make a telephone call, when Margaret interrupted and told her that she was driving her to the hospital.

Two hours later they returned and Margaret finished the story. The hospital doctor had examined Johanna's bite—definitely that of a black widow spider—and said that only the day before a man had been admitted into the emergency room with anaphylactic shock from a similar bite. The medical workup on Johanna, however, showed no reaction.

"The spider's dead and you are fine. This is the first time I have seen no reaction to such a bite, but I guess there is no reason for you to stay. You are free to leave now," concluded the doctor.

While Johanna was for the first time dealing with a

typical immune system, Margaret who had never been in perfect health was experiencing all the usual side effects of chemotherapy. So in the midst of the humiliation and the money problems, both were sick. Margaret's surgery was a success and the chemo was working. The Mini-Reformer, or the Body Former by Pilates, was also a success. Monthly sales were in the thousands. Thousands of units. The dollars would run into the millions. With the added revenues from the videos and the accessories and the workout clothes, her little mini was turning into a Pilates empire. A tunnel into Fort Knox for the trademark gang.

Although the success of the Mini on home shopping should have validated Johanna's idea, her losing it to the trademark gang showed everyone that she didn't understand how the game was played. No one cared about ideas, about creativity. The only pride was that of ownership. Margaret could easily blame Johanna for the cancer and the financial failure, too. And, for turning her passion for Pilates into pain.

Johanna now knows that she can no longer look at a glass that's half empty and say that it's half full. Now, the glass is broken. There is nothing to be optimistic about.

20

ANOTHER GOODBYE

"If you're looking for an exercise regimen that increases strength and balance, engages your mind and body, and makes you look great without adding bulk to your muscles, then The Pilates Method...could work for you."
—New York Post, 1998

Johanna floated in Guy's pool and attempted to shut down her thoughts. The warm sun, the cool water, even Guy himself could not distract her brain from entwining itself around her business dilemmas. It was all becoming a bit chronic. Maybe Pilates in the pool was a new direction they should consider. She thought about standing exercises using water as resistance. She tried again to stop thinking, resolving to relax. No point in wasting the pleasure of a lovely day that she so desperately needed. Surrounded by a stunning setting with the sexiest man alive, and she is trying to figure out how to market exercises. Forcing herself to tune out Pilates, she saw Guy's housekeeper coming poolside carrying a heavy Nambe silver tray with lunch. Realizing that she was hungry, always a good sign, she got out of the pool with an appetite and joined Guy for a salad of shrimp remoulade, her favorite Vouvray wine, some locally made cheeses and fruit. Finally beginning to chill, she imagined herself transported to the south of France. She carried two glasses of wine over to the chaise where Guy already lay and joined him for some sun bathing.

After who knows how long, she awoke to see Guy's glistening body on the pool lounge floating around in the water. Johanna watched his eyes close. When his mat drifted toward her side of the pool, she got up, set down her sunglasses, walked to the pool's edge and slipped in. Surfacing alongside of Guy, she removed his sunglasses and grabbed his thigh.

"No," he said. "One mustn't swim so soon after eating. Don't you know that?"

"Rules, Guy, are for the guidance of wise men and the obedience of fools."

With a swift tug, she pulled him beneath the water. They swam together to the far end where they rested on the tile pool steps.

After a long smoldering look, the type that made French films so distracting, he led her out of the pool. They made their way to the cabana where Guy, a most charming host, slowly dried her bare, wet skin with a thick towel, a lovely warm up to what this Frenchman believed was the preferred form of exercise.

Afterward Johanna relaxed fully and let the rest of the glorious afternoon pass undisturbed by her constantly percolating mind. She dreamily envisioned them at Cap Ferrat together, drinking champagne and eating langoustine by the pool. She, of course, had a fabulous white turban Turkish towel thing going on about her head which set off her golden tan and perfect Chanel Rouge pedicure.

She awoke to find Guy sitting, reading beside her. Rested, but without skipping a beat, her mind filled with earlier thoughts.

"I can't believe it's taken me this long to figure it out," she told him.

"That I am exquisite and you're staying for dinner?" he said.

"Yes to both, of course. But do you want me to stay? I am so preoccupied with work problems. You are, were, divine. But presently I am swimming with constant thoughts and only myself for counsel."

"You may share these thoughts, Johanna. I will listen if it will keep you here a bit longer."

"It's stupid, but if they hadn't taken my Mini-Reformer, I would be nearing completion of my mission. Instead I have to reinvent the Institute again. Do you know that American expression, "Turning lemons into lemonade?"

"No. Tell me in French."

"Avec des citrons faisons d'un citron presse ou une limonade."

"Ah, mais oui, avec sucre. Sugar is money in business. You need dough as you Americans say to fix the problem."

"You French are so cynical. I believe that in working through a problem and in trying to solve it you can come upon a better way. Discover an idea that you wouldn't have thought of."

"In French we call this naiveté."

"Is this why some people say that the French have cornered the market on cynicism?"

"That expression is on the subject of arrogance, and you know it."

"I still love you and the other 50 million arrogant Frenchmen. Call me a Pollyanna which I know you think I am." He nodded in agreement.

"Anyway, about my new epiphany which is that the The Institute's reinvention should center around the Pilates matwork. With our Fundamentals, it can be the next evolution," she proposed becoming more excited upon hearing the idea spoken out loud. Pilates clients don't really know it. Many Pilates teachers can't teach it. So that's an opportunity, right? There are 20,000 health clubs with millions of members. Right now Americans only do Pilates in private studios on the apparatus. I can develop a special certification program. Look at yoga. It is growing so fast because you don't need machines. Thousands of group exercise teachers in health clubs can add Pilates matwork."

She was now standing, then pacing, tempted to jump up and down. "This is my ticket back," she enthused. "This may really pay some of the bills. This is going to be one hell of a new beginning."

Guy set down his book, reached for her hand and then pulled her back onto the bed. He pressed his sleek suntanned body against her. But his mind seemed as far away as France.

"What's wrong?" she said.

He took her hand and kissed it. "To new beginnings," he whispered.

Johanna dressed to leave. The house phone had rung too many times to be ignored any longer. Guy, too much the gentleman to remove himself, had called out to his housemaid repeatedly in his own Franco-Spanish language. It was time to wrap this beautiful interlude. Guy slipped on a robe and walked Johanna to the Miata.

"I'm off to Paris tomorrow afternoon," he said. "I m not sure for how long."

He pushed back Johanna's sunglasses and kissed her forehead. They exchanged a few French goodbyes. Johanna drove out the driveway and picked up speed on Bishop's Lodge Road. She wanted the wind in her damp hair and the radio too loud. She looked out her rear view mirror at the Tesuque hills. Like the pleasures of this perfect day, they were receding behind her. She would hold this memory and trust the insights she had shared.

Guy had not said how long he would be gone. She was unsure what message his eyes had tried to convey.

21

LEGAL SAGA—*TURNING POINT*

"A mainstay in the arena of dance medicine and gaining quickly in sports medicine, Pilates has officially gone mainstream: Such diverse publications as **Glamour, USA Today,** *and* **Men's Fitness** *have declared it the "in" exercise of 1999."*

—**Biomechanics, 1999**

"First we kill all the lawyers" —*Polipher's speech, Henry the Fifth, Shakespeare*

From the start, legal issues had clouded the excitement of starting the Institute. For five years, Johanna had felt as if she were Gross' favorite piñata. From the time the Institute opened its doors, the media recognized Johanna as the go to source for Pilates information. And as the Institute gained a reputation as the bright star in the Pilates firmament, Gross recognized too that he was benefiting from Johanna's work and vision: more publicity for Pilates, meant a bigger business for him. Still the legal attacks continued and constantly eclipsed the excitement Johanna felt when something went right. Moments of elation, such as when Will at Nortrax first demonstrated the Mini-Reformer prototype, always were quickly followed by bruising disappointment, such as when Will's boss called off the Nortrax deal mere hours after being contacted by the trademark gang's attorney.

Defending against the legal assaults drained away the Institute's resources and energy and caused it to employ so many lawyers, who had accomplished so little, that Johanna sardonically joked that the Institute had become a non-profit job creation program for attorneys. For the most part, Johanna handled her growing resentment of the legal profession civilly. There were moments, however, when she wanted a license to kill, such as when their fourth lawyer, who had filed their Trademark Cancellation Action in Washington, called her after a year's wait to say that the Judges had refused to rule, so the trademark still stood.

"Relax Johanna, everything is okay, we've bought time," David, Lawyer Four blithely told her.

She could not comprehend or tolerate his noncha-lance. "Whose time was bought?" Johanna demanded. "Well surely your time, and now we bought time for Gross to increase his branding, to strengthen his position, to demolish the competition. Don't you guys get it, it's a race." Johanna snapped. "We don't need time! You know how races are won—in the shortest time!"

Up until 1996, Johanna was not the sole victim of the legal attacks, she was just the biggest target. Even small Pilates studios were at risk. They found that local publicity was both a blessing and a curse, as it alerted the trademark attorneys to their existence, and promptly brought forth cease and desist orders.

Lawsuits are great default tactics for those who can't put together a smart business plan. The trademark legal team was sending several trees worth of cease and desist orders to Pilates teachers everywhere. In the early years of the legal battle, a Pilates teacher's first call, after receiving a legal letter, was to the Institute. Long conversations with Johanna about legal options were followed by Forum articles with more technicalities supplied by Institute lawyers. The Institute had emboldened studios to use the name, which meant, unfortunately, that some came to blame the Institute for their legal woes.

These teachers and studios turned away from the Institute's leadership. They quickly forgot that before the legal letters there weren't any clients either. When the Institute caved on the name, Gross could taste victory. He bragged there was only one more Pilates business to take down: Kent Hemel's Pilates apparatus manufacturing business.

Big mistake.

The nation-sweeping proliferation of Pilates studios,

fueled by the media, meant boom times for Hemel. Still based in California, Hemel's company had quietly, but quickly grown to something worth suing over. Now doing business on both coasts and even Europe, Hemel was the biggest planet in the Pilates universe. When Gross sued him for trademark infringement in 1996, Hemel—after watching Gross bully other Pilates players for years—girded for battle.

Gross suddenly found himself playing with the big boys. Not only did Hemel counter-sue, he had the suit certified as a class action.

While Johanna would have much preferred that Hemel had agreed to an alliance years before, which might have prevented Gross from getting off the ground, she was grateful he finally joined the fray. Now, he had a chance to be Superman. Or maybe to wrest the 'heavy hitter Pilates champion of the world' title from Gross, who had worn it unchallenged for too long. Hemel was now ready for a face off in the big ring: the Southern District Court of New York.

Class action status meant the entire Pilates community could get behind the effort to fight the Gross menace. The entire Pilates community that is, except for the Institute. Since they had already settled, their position was 'compromised.' Yet ironically, their second lawsuit, the Mini-Reformer patent infringement suit, was the one-two punch that would help topple Gross' trademark. Johanna knew that if one corner of her office had legal documents stacked to the ceiling, Gross —now facing a well-funded class action and his partners the Institute infringement suit—could be pushed out of his office by paper. He'd probably have to rent a large storage locker, maybe two.

Meanwhile, since Pilates had been zooming in popularity while the legal clashes raged, Pilates teachers who had been justifiably frightened by the legalese, could now turn their focus from the courts to their jam-packed studios. Clients were streaming in. Teachers who hadn't rotated their springs in five years were ordering replacements.

Johanna had jump-started an industry, taking it from a cult to an expanding niche, promoting a word and a method that just a few years before practically no one knew, and few could pronounce. Now it was recognized. Not a household name, but on its way.

Of course, the irony was that now Johanna's Institute was unable to take advantage of the class action suit that was protecting individual studios. Her fight for survival was still uphill. Though her Institute had originated the model for professional Pilates training, she couldn't certify the teachers she instructed as 'Pilates' trainers. She couldn't use this name on their certificates.

Still, she thought that she could revitalize the

Institute by adding other modalities. She had swung from believing the forced name change to the BodyMind Institute was an opportunity to fearing it was fatal then back to seeing its benefits. The Institute could, she now believed, cross-reference and popularize other still esoteric techniques in order to truly develop a place for bodymind awareness. Was this taking on too much? Would others be interested in this type of intellectual partnership? Had others delving into different body therapies reached the same conclusion? Bodymind was no longer a niche. It was a category. Maybe fusion was her new ticket. How about Feldenkreis and Pilates. Feldenlates. Maybe in Israel.

This time around she didn't waste too much time and energy on her cross-pollination idea. As she already suspected, none of the body gurus from other disciplines were interested in partnership with the Institute. Her problems were too well known and served as a cautionary tale for others. Watching the Pilates legal mess, they rushed to hire their own legal experts. Confidentiality agreements followed like lactic acid build-up. Then trademarks. And patents. Certification hierarchies with their own master teachers and complicated codes of entry completed the package.

Although Johanna was a pragmatist, she had too easily been seduced by New Age rhetoric. The talk of community and sharing. The commitment to an ideal beyond competing for a bigger share. Now, she had to admit to herself, she had been foolishly idealistic. She should have been a business guru, not a healing one. Back alone on her Italian couch, she was abruptly snapped out of her recriminations by the ringing of her new cell phone.

"Guess what, you are not alone anymore. It's contagious." Johanna was relieved to hear Meredith's voice. "A friend told me that Rolfers have been doing battle, too. Even though Ida Rolf's will specified who, what, where, and when there's been some sort of rift. Two of her Master teachers have split off and formed their own group."

"That news has also reached us here in Santa Fe," Johanna observed dryly. "Something about who can use the term rolfer. Trademark lawyers are encircling Boulder. Who knew these transcendental 'masters' could muster up some good old Western Civ for ruthless self-preservation."

"So come home. New York style beats New Age mode any time."

"I've got just a little work left here to finish. But I have been figuring out an escape plan. Moving the business to New York, even for me—your get-on-with-it-no-nonsense friend—is a big, big job. Although I do have a plan. I'm just 2000 miles and mucho dollars short of re-entry. I know I'm right about the Pilates matwork potential. And with the right training program and little bit of luck, I'm there. The health clubs are going to find it extremely appealing. Extremely. This is my last big hurrah for the Land before Time, excuse me, the Land of Enchantment. Then it's you and me in line at Dean and Deluca."

"Well, hurry. While you are saving the American core out West I'm busy here saving my sanity. Salmon, smoked or fresh, will be in short supply if another diet or skin expert gets interviewed by the *Post* about its miracle properties."

22

THE MATWORK

"There's a reason celebrities love it and gyms are scrambling to offer classes. Who doesn't want to look taller and slimmer? It's hard to decide what's more impressive about Pilates: the claims... or the celebrity clientele (Madonna, Uma Thurman and Julia Roberts)."
—**Weight Watchers Magazine, 1998**

N ow in her eighth lesson with Rebecca Sanson, Johanna sat on an ordinary hard-backed chair and concentrated on releasing. Letting go of decades of tension that had lodged in her bones, in her muscles, while registering twenty body checkpoints. Rebecca, a certified teacher of the Alexander Technique, was also a Teacher Trainer, an Educational Presenter, and a Master. Body people loved these designations. Johanna found them too Eastern mumbo jumbo for her taste. The only black belt she believed in, an Yves St. Laurent, circa 1987, was hanging in her closet.

Whenever Johanna thought about these training pyramids, a favorite Noel Coward quip popped into her mind. Noel was recovering from surgery 'in hospital' as they say on the other side of the pond, and a visiting friend counseled that when returning home, he must hire a trained nurse. To which Coward replied, "What the hell would I do with an untrained nurse?"

Johanna knew that she shouldn't let these irreverent thoughts intrude when she was trying to go deeper into the temple that was her body. She should be free instead to consciously concentrate on her previously unconscious movements. Focusing again she slid her butt far back so as to touch the chair's junction between seat and backrest. Then, by following Rebecca's soothing voice instructing her every move, she rose up to standing "effortlessly." This supposedly natural movement required bending forward at the hip joint, simultaneously connecting her abdominals, opening her chest, lengthening her neck, releasing her jaw, freeing her head, externally rotating her biceps, grounding her feet, while remembering always to inhale and exhale rhythmically.

Rebecca, with hushed reverence, explained how Frederick Mathias Alexander developed his Technique. Alexander was an Australian Shakespearean actor who stepped on stage one day circa 1898, opened his mouth and only a hoarse sound emerged. He spent the next decades researching why his voice croaked on stage. He determined that our buried stuff, our inner demons could inhibit correct function. Johanna's get-on-with-it mind couldn't help thinking what if his mother had just said: "*Fred, don't clench. And definitely don't slouch.*" After identifying his problem, Alexander became his first subject in his search to devise a solution. It was a similar story with the other body Masters. Pilates had rheumatic fever and a scrawny body and Feldenkreis a knee injury. Each one evolved elaborate body methods that attracted a following of body junkies who became students, then teacher trainees, shadowing the Master to absorb his truths. After the Master passed into a Heaven where all bodies are perfect, these devoted teachers fought to claim the crown. Different camps emerged, each one convinced that they were the only ones who could represent the Master's philosophy.

Johanna had tried the Alexander Technique in New York 15 years ago with the teacher, Joanne Anold, recommended as the best, more than a master teacher, a master commander. Even though she found the experience very enjoyable, she didn't continue, a typical pattern she learned. Even body junkies, which she was not, start and stop and start again.

"Yes," Rebecca said. "It isn't that people don't have the time, or money, or interest, for that matter. You have to be ready for it."

"I've heard all about it some New Age explanation of how "one must come to it" upon reaching some other mystical developmental stage. A perfect place where all parts of oneself are brought together. Ohm," said Johanna.

"In America, this awareness is harder than it should be," explained Rebecca. "You've heard the story that émigrés from England fell into two categories. The criminals were

were sent to Australia and the Puritans fled to America. This could explain why it has taken so long in America for bodymind integration to be recognized. Pilates took decades to become popular. Maybe the Alexander Technique will follow."

"It's why we Yankees punish our bodies with deprivation diets and all pain, no gain exercise. Or that while we totally lack body awareness, we're drowning in self-absorption. That's the American way," said Johanna.

"You are being too hard on everyone. The success of Pilates shows that people are open to renewal. Just as you are. We can all go deeper and renew."

Rebecca   reminded   Johanna   of   Margaret. Similar styles. With their reverent tones, regal posture, and composure, they could have been sisters. When Margaret left the Institute for good last month, she said it was to distance herself from Pilates. She was laying blame on the lawsuits, betrayals, stress, financial problems, and a hundred other miseries. She felt isolated from her prior community. She had come to hate it all, her exact words.

Not that Johanna didn't understand the desire for distance. She needed a vacation from Pilates, too, which is why she had decided to revisit Alexander. And to sample some of the others. In Santa Fe it was easy. Every mind-body therapy was there. Some that practically no one knew about like Aston Patterning, Trager, Polarity, Reiki. They had their Master teachers and certification workshops. Santa Fe was the perfect place to focus inward. The problem was that no one then wanted to go outward. To see the big picture. The forest and the trees. Connecting the dots.

Later, back alone in the stillness of the late afternoon, Johanna recognized again that the Pilates matwork development was crucial to the Institute's survival. This time she wouldn't have to convince her partners. She was it. It was up to her to develop the program, not that she hadn't contributed mightily to their existing one. But Margaret—with Eve's counsel—had assumed the role of subject matter expert. She was a brilliant teacher. Knew every exercise and their biomechanics, too. But without Johanna's experience in educational publishing, including several years writing programmed learning instruction, and then another decade responsible for the training of a few thousand hairdressers, program development would have taken years. Together they were a great team. Margaret knew the material. She knew training protocols and course development. Plus she could write.

Johanna pushed herself to take apart every matwork exercise. No pacing around someone else. She didn't have to wait now. She just had to do it. But, still she wanted some support. Some interaction. Not partners anymore. Just another voice—preferably one that knew something— that could tell her she was on track. She thought about the Certifying Studio teachers. Could they help her? They were the ones who would ultimately do the training. Maybe, but maybe they would just parrot back whatever they had heard at their last workshop given by some Master teacher. She needed to go elsewhere and suddenly she knew where that was.

Jacqueline Kane, she decided, was the person who could help her. She had met her years ago in New York at the Pilates Studio at Bendel's. A former dancer, she was teaching Pilates there and trying to figure out her next move. Did she stay and maybe get the Director position? Did she wait and then open her own studio?

She finally decided neither one would work. First, there was the trademark problem, which in New York was too close to ignore. Then there were the unanswered anatomical questions. Or questions that no one wanted to answer. So she decided to become a physical thera- pist. Better yet, one who understood movement and knew Pilates. The best of both with no legal hassles. And immediately she got her degree at Columbia, trained with Marta Miller, the renowned Physical Therapist in the field of Dance Medicine, married and moved to Miami, far away from the New York-based trademark gang. Years later when Johanna opened the Institute, Jacqueline had joined to support her and so they had kept in touch. She was the perfect person to phone for an honest opinion about the matwork idea.

"So how's the weather? Must be hot, " Johanna asked.

"Only outside. We live in air conditioned 'comfort' here. You know how much I hate that. So bad for the body," Jacqueline responded.

"It's perfect no-humidity weather here. My guest casita is yours. And by the way, I am trying to design a matwork certification. I am bored talking to myself and I'm not sure I know where to start."

"So the program will be to train instructors to teach the matwork. In studios or health clubs?"

"Both, but the big market is really the Clubs. There are thousands. They always need new programming."

"Absolutely, plus their group exercise teachers are ready to lie down after years of aerobic jumping. They'd welcome Joe's work."

"Yes but most of these people just learned to pronounce Pilates. They have never been in a room with a
Reformer. Their cues are more like cheers. "Go girl, go.""

"And that's why you are the perfect person to do this
Jacqueline told her. You're the one who figured out that
there are really only nine spinal exercises, not 500. The
Institute already teaches the seven Modification principles,
and the Fundamentals, now all you have to do is teach the
major body types and then how to put it together."

"But if it is so logical, why haven't other Pilates
teachers done it?"

"And why do you waste energy trying to figure them
out? Some just don't want to think it through. Others believe
they must do it exactly as Joe did it even though by this
time who really knows what that is. His Method has
been passed on for so long verbally that it is almost like the
telephone game."

Johanna played along. "Is it a neutral spine or
tucked, and which one did Joe teach?"

"Sure that is our defining issue—what separates us from the them. I have photos of Joe working in a tucked position and I have seen others where he was teaching someone and her spine was in neutral. I know that he would be teaching neutral if he were here today. This battle is so tired."

"Ok, but indulge me with one more. Since Pilates teachers have great body awareness, why doesn't the Roberta camp feel that the abdominals work better in neutral?"

"Because contrary to what you want to believe, dancers don't all have perfect bodies. They have their own imbalances and compensations. You have always glorified them. Then they don't live up and you are so disappointed. And maybe it is something else entirely. Just a version of that Australian saying."

"The one about the criminals?"

"No. The one about when someone climbs the ladder, they pull it up so the next person has to climb higher. Maybe they do question the tucked position, but they are already certified by Roberta and they don't want to start again with new information."

"I just dropped the ladder. Did you hear it fall? So my next step should be a syllabus with the Fundamentals, Modification and Variation principles, Major Body Types, and how to break down and teach the first 25 mat exercises. What else?"

"You need to go deeper with the pelvis, male/female differences, breathing and the pelvic floor. Do a first draft and send it to me."

"I am going to video teaching the postural info too so you can get the total enchilada."

"I'll take a Margarita also? There's not much New Mexican cuisine here, but we have lots of great Cuban places. What I am really missing is snow and skiing. I haven't been in almost seven years."

"Now here's a deal you can't refuse. My goal is to get this course done and then transmit it to our Certifying Studios early next year. In late March, let's say. Just when Spring skiing is beginning. Lots of powder. Please come out here and help me teach it to the 40 Pilates teachers who will come here so they can offer this course. Your PT, dance and, of course, Pilates credentials will keep them inline. If I try this alone they may gang up on me. And I have had enough with that other gang."

"This is a deal that I can't refuse. Have you tried the new parabolic skis yet? I hear that they practically turn by themselves."

"They do, but I am not skiing much now. I took up Argentine tango and now I am afraid that if I fall and then get injured... You know what I mean. I am getting as crazy as you dancers now that I am hooked on tango."

"Yeah, loving to dance has its dark side. But you'll be ok on the slopes, the dance floor, and in the studio. I'll help you. If I have any questions, I'lll ask Marta. She knows everything about the body and she wants you to succeed. You can talk to both of us.. You still have plenty of supporters. And friends too."

"Gracias. Especially for the last part. I'm taking off my tango shoes and going to the mat. And there will be some surprises, too. Besides tango, I've also fallen for the Alexander Technique, which is helping my Pilates workout. I'm going to rethink how we cue so that the body has more ease, more length. And to extend the focus from the core so we cover more real estate, meaning more of the body. So you'll have a lot to check."

After her confirming conversation with Jacqueline, Johanna was totally ready to redirect and restart. She could do it, had always done it. She put her racing mind and racing body in check. Ok, maybe she was only pacing a bit now, but she was just warming up. She was positioned to move forward. The Institute had its membership and 40 well-placed Certifying Studios. The logical next step was to dust off the Pilates matwork and get it out there. Not one-on-one, but in groups. And the beauty of it? Clubs and gyms would be clamoring for Pilates training, thus becoming a part of this exclusive fitness method. Matwork Certification would be their entry ticket. She couldn't wait to talk with Meredith. She picked up the phone, but put it back down. It could wait, after all, she needed as her Alexander teacher had said, to renew. She renewed again for another 30 seconds and then dialed Meredith. She was several steps closer to coming home.

23

THE CHAIR

"Pilates exercises and their derivatives are performed either on a padded floor mat or with special equipment. While on the mat, the body supplies its own resistance to movement, by way of gravity. ...even a single session can relieve muscle stress and leave you feeling more aware of your body."
Harvard Women's Health Watch, 1999

L ate one chilly April evening in 1999, Johanna, alone as usual, lay on a Reformer in the empty studio focusing on some mental spring cleaning with a little exercise sprinkled in. She cherry-picked her way through her favorite supine exercises from Footwork through Short Spine. She repeated a silly saying, originally referencing wine, that she had converted for her favorite exercise, 'a day without Short Spine is like a day without Sunshine.'

Thirty minutes spent in just this way was familiar, comfortable, even comforting. What it wasn't was a workout for her dear old mind and body. After several decades working out in this way, she usually slipped into autopilot after the first ten minutes. With her body moving, but mind detached, or somewhat detached, she thought of the Reformer as Old Reliable. The Cadillac, although special, was never for her the main event. Except for the tiny Wunda Chair, Pilates apparatus was all super-sized. The Pilates legend had it that Joe designed the Wunda Chair for dancer Ted Shawn so he could take it with him to the Jacob's Pillow Dance Festival in Massachusetts. Joe, realizing he had a 'winner' because of its small size, its portability, announced that his Chair would soon make its way into every Home, Hotel, and Hospital. None of this happened, of course. It never even made it into many actual Pilates studios, and even those few rarely used it.

For her own edification, Johanna decided to revisit the Wunda Chair's history. Maybe she would learn something that had been overlooked all these years. She relearned the related exercises and played with the suggested resistance. She tried to find a spring resistance pattern as she had years ago with the Reformer. She studied the dimensions. The design, from an aesthetic perspective, was, as in all Joe's inventions, not a priority. But this piece not only looked like a prototype, it looked like his first and only! She knew the name had to go. Wunda, German slang for wonder, wouldn't work here. It lacked name recognition, anyway. And, speaking of names, there was no trademark. She could redesign it, rename it and add Health clubs to his "H" list: Health Clubs, Homes, Hotels, and Hospitals. It sounded right. How had she overlooked the Chair when rethinking the apparatus on the first go around? Thanks for asking. The thing was already sized right, but nothing else about it worked. The fact that it was an ugly, squat, wooden box with no sex appeal, were among the obvious reasons why it had been ignored. Good. Let the competition fight over redesigning Reformers. Let them try to re-engineer the Cadillac. For once, she was going to keep an idea of hers a secret.

Johanna knew that she could rename the Chair and fix its aesthetics, but fixing its design problems was not going to be a cakewalk. The exercises didn't feel right. The flow and the range were limited. The spring attachments were not just irritating, they were impossible. During the months that she worked with the Chair, she swore she had broken every fingernail on both hands. If she managed to hook the springs so they were secure, then she couldn't unhook them without a battle. While struggling with them, strands of her hair would get trapped in the springs. Talk about a bad hair day. So far this was very short of a 'wonder' machine. The foot bar was way too narrow. The 'ride' was short and jerky, its range of motion limited by the position of the springs. At present, Joe's baby had absolutely nothing going for it except its small size. But the Chair exercises were important. Many were weight bearing. Even sweat producing. Not wimpy. They deserved a better platform.

Pacing the studio, Johanna's brain went into over-drive trying to think of some engineering type to work it all out. Clients, tango class acquaintances, neighborhood meetings, her kids' friend's parents—a steady stream of faces passed before her. As she rummaged in her bag for an emery board to file down another nail, an image popped into her head. A pair of eyes, actually. Two pale blue eyes belonging to. . . . What was his name?

Lloyd, that was it. Lloyd Something-or-other. She'd met him at the tennis club last month. Tall, blonde, with a homespun Midwestern accent. Shy though, earnestly shy. He'd blushed slightly when the tennis pro had introduced them. Lloyd was an engineer working at Los Alamos, or Sandia. One of the local national laboratories keeping America safe. They had only chatted briefly. He wasn't a club member, but was there to play in a tournament. She had been struck by how ill-at-ease he seemed among the wealthy trust funders and rich Texan club members. Well, she wasn't going out with him, she just needed his expert advice. Re-engineering an exercise machine would be like playing in a sandbox compared to whatever he did up on the hill, or wherever.

She had been right about Lloyd. He had sounded very interested in the project and in finding out more. Or so he said when she phoned him. Once in the studio, it became clear that 'the more' might be her.

Lee and Johanna were just coming back to the Institute from a trip to Santa Fe Subscription when Johanna saw Lloyd on Palace Avenue looking for their building.

"Lee, what's the time? There he is," Johanna said

"Good work!" He's a sexy hunk," Lee said quickly.

"Are you serious? Oh, he's so, too earnest. Not sexy, not my type at all."

"What is your type, Johanna?"

"Guy."

"Huh, I like my type *in town.*" Lee shrugged her shoulders wondering if Johanna could take a joke.

"Good one, Lee. It's been eight months."

Johanna walked hastily inside and up the stairs. Changing into a black backless Unitard, just in case, she greeted him as he waited in the studio looking totally uncomfortable.

"Sorry to keep you waiting, but I put on exercise clothes so I could show you that this dumb-looking box has a reason to exist," Johanna said trying to get him interested. While Johanna demo-ed a few choice exercises on the Chair, Lloyd scrutinized the spring attachments or just stared. His brow furrowed in concentration. He pushed gently on the foot pedal to test its tension.

"So you... you... want to replace the springs with

bungees?" His face reddened as he kept his eyes away from Johanna's leg movements.

"Well," Johanna said. "That's what is on the Mini-Reformer. Of course, that is only a retail product. He nodded and looked directly at her.

"Is that a problem?" she said.

"No," he said. "No. I was just wondering if…" His voice trailed off as he walked around to the other side of the Chair and bent down to examine the springs underneath.

Not her type. Very much like those clean-cut astronauts in *The Right Stuff*. But those pale blue eyes. And a really terrific body…

Weeks later, or eight business meetings later, they decided to discuss the Chair's progress at Ten Thousand Waves Spa one evening after work. Lloyd was nearly finished with the first working prototype of the Chair and wanted to present it afterward at his place. This fact became a mantra he repeated as they drove through the downtown area and out Bishops Lodge Road towards the spa. Johanna tried to will the car forward, toward memories that were still circling Tesuque and Guy. The car jerked right pushing her out of her reverie as Lloyd raced the light onto Artist Road and began the climb towards the Sangre de Cristo mountains.

A posted sign read 'Ski Basin 17 miles.' Johanna sensed the depth, felt the rush of complete darkness enveloping them as they continued driving. A few minutes farther and a small glowing light on the left led into the spa's entrance. Johanna and Meredith, when she had visited, had gone to "The Waves" for outdoor soaking, a salt scrub, massage and a seaweed wrap. Johanna had never been there with a man, but thought her suggestion not overly forward considering Lloyd's diffidence. She felt in control. She could swing it either way.

In a Japanese-style cedar paneled room they lay on adjacent tables as two female masseurs worked deeply into their bones. Sounds of waterfalls and cedar scents wafted in the air. The physical sensation of unwinding was opening her to the possibilities. But when she glanced over at Lloyd, his face serene, his eyes closed blissfully, she couldn't read him. Later, wrapped in thick white robes, they retired to the Kobuta outdoor bath. Standing on the wooden slats surrounding the small pool, she slipped off her robe and stepped first into the night air and then lowered herself into the steaming water. The bath faced the lights of Santa Fe below and was shaded by a wooden awning. As she slid her salt-scrubbed naked body into its warm embrace, she felt surprisingly comfortable. Glancing up, she spotted Lloyd, wrapped securely in his robe, running his hand over the wood working detail of the bath's enclosure. It was dark and they hadn't seen each other naked yet. She tried to find his manner endearing. She closed her eyes and leaned her head back against the edge of the tub to give him some privacy. After a moment's silence, she heard the robe drop to the wooden floor. She let him slip privately into the tub's edge across from her. When she opened her eyes, he was facing away, looking into the night sky.

After soaking a while, Johanna, having decided not to linger, asked, "Are you getting hungry? We should be going soon if we hope to get a bite in town, you know every-thing closes up by nine."

"I don't usually eat a complete dinner though."

"No?" she said.

"I like to graze," he said. "Six small meals a day. It's much healthier."

"Really?" she said. "Interesting."

Johanna asked herself what she doing in an oversized bath tub with this guy talking about his healthy eating habits.   Next he would tell her how much water he drank. And what brand. So this was the new evolved man. This is what women's lib had wrought. Men obsessing about their health.   Christ, this didn't do anything to get one's juices flowing. If he didn't have an appetite, what did that indicate about other pleasures? Sitting naked in the Kobuta bath

bath with only half of their date over, she realized that—that was that. Lloyd and she had no future of a personal nature.

Lloyd was a good engineer. Just not her style of design. Months into the project and he remained permanently "nearly finished." Johanna finally realized he didn't want to finish. But with her constant glass half full point of view, she did learn something about spring resistance that no one else seemed to know.

"It's the bungees, Johanna," he said to her while picking at a Tupperware container full of raw carrots and broccoli as he kneeled on the carpet in the studio the following week. He pointed to the springs under the original Wunda Chair.

"I tried to mimic the precise action of spring tension with bungee cords and it doesn't work."

"Doesn't work?" she said, "but that's what they've used in the Mini-Reformer."

He shook his head. "Not the same. Springs are different from bungees. The spring's force production curve is not only precisely linear, but its curve increases more thus producing more resistance. The bungees curve is flatter. It's technical."

"I'm listening," she said kneeling down next to him. She

hated when he assumed she couldn't understand basic engineering concepts. He reached over the top of the Chair and pressed down on one of the foot pedals with his large hand.

"See here? With a spring, the more you stretch it, the stronger the tension. Also springs have relatively little inertia. The 'input' force trying to return the spring from a stretched to a contracted position is applied by the spring itself. As a result, the return of a freely contracting spring is relatively instantaneous. Bungees have some of these properties, but they can't duplicate them exactly because they have a different rate of stretch at almost every point. And they deteriorate very quickly so whatever they feel like in the beginning will change very soon. Well-made springs will keep the rate of stretch/resistance for a much longer period of time. In fact, the bungee deterioration rate may be as high as 75% faster than that of a spring."

She sat back on her heels and stared at the action of the pedal stressing the springs as he repeated the motion. "So bungee won't work. I should have surmised this because Margaret was never comfortable with them. She said that the feel was different," Johanna said realizing that some manufacturing expert should have known these technical differences.

"As I said, bungees suffer from greater hysteresis as they return from a stretched to a neutral condition. Hysteresis is energy that is lost during contraction due to internal friction among the fibers that make up the elastic member.   Since energy is lost, the force pulling the cord back is at slightly lower force than the extension. In Pilates, the extension is as important as the linear force."

And they were marketing her Mini-Reformer with bungees, not springs. Perhaps only rocket scientists knew this technical stuff.

"Very interesting," she said.

Part 3
The Present 2000-today

Pilates nearly 60   Jan. 1940

"In less than ten years Pilates has gone from not even being on the radar to a mainstream exercise practice. The number of studios and people participating in Pilates has grown exponentially. In 1991, there were a handful of studios... Today in 2006, there are 5,000."

—IDEA Fitness, 2006

24

VICTORY

"What's in a name? You can now say the P-word. Last year, a federal court declared Pilates a generic term, much like karate or yoga... the method became much sought after ...it became known that many Hollywood celebrities used Pilates in their own workout regimens."
—Club Industry Magazine, 2001

After a decade spent jump-starting Pilates, Johanna still couldn't accept the clichés applauding procrastination. *Haste makes waste. Slow and steady wins the race. Patience is a virtue. The wheels of justice turn slowly.* After five long years of legal machinations that cost millions of dollars, many of them hers, a New York judge finally handed down a landmark decision which proved conclusively that because of abandonment and generic usage, the Pilates mark was cancelled. The stunning victory on those counts made an appeal impossible. Everything, including use, registration, and protection of the so-called Pilates trademark had been mishandled all along. Seven years after the Institute's Cancellation of Trademark action was filed and then ignored by the Trademark Court, the legal system couldn't avoid a ruling any longer. Too many businesses, too many individual livelihoods had been in limbo too long. Dozens of studio owners had been sued; thousands received threatening cease and desist letters. But on October 19, 2000 it was finally over. The Pilates name had been liberated.

Several days after the news of the victory, Meredith telephoned Johanna to get the juicy details and to give her a reality check. "They never wanted you to demystify Pilates. Now that the coast is clear, let's see who comes crawling out of the woodwork. There will be new masters, and certifiers, and equipment firms across the land. New alliances and new royalty."

Sitting alone in her too-spacious house, Johanna listened to Meredith wisely call it for what it was.

"You should bring the business back home," Meredith said.

"We've been there before, Meredith," she said. "You don't know how tempting that is."

"So?"

Johanna picked up the remote control from the coffee table and started flicking through the channels with the sound muted as Meredith continued her pitch.

"You want the truth?" Meredith said.

"No," she lied.

"Truth is that the second coming of Pilates may be too late to save American bodies. The 'exercise more' directive has failed them. Obesity is practically epidemic. Don't be so sure that these bodies can be resurrected with just your beloved Pilates. I see fat-burning exercise sneaking around the corner."

"Meredith, your words are jumping off the TV screen. Hold that thought. I am turning up the volume. Turn on your TV. Go to the Shopping channel. Ok, it's starting. You've got the right channel? Look at her. She's on," Johanna shouted.

It was Buffy selling the Mini-Reformer/Body Former on the Shopping Network.

"Who's that?" Meredith asked.

"Buffy!" she said. "Who else? Oh, Meredith, can you believe this?!"

Johanna watched Buffy, all smiles and angelic blonde hair demonstrate the awesome versatility of the Body Former to her breathless hostess, Donna.

"And the best part, Donna," she said. "Is the new aerobic feature."

Meredith returned to the phone. "TV shopping,

never thought it would come to this," she murmured.

"That is the woman who gave Pilates to the masses in her own words," Johanna said. "Look at this performance. They've remade the Pilates Jump Board and now it is bouncy."

On the screen, Buffy attached a two-foot square board at the foot bar, and then lying down on the carriage with her feet pressed against it she pushed off. "You see this, Donna?" she said. "There is no stress whatsoever on my spine or my knees."

Like a pinball shooting out of its spring-loaded berth, Buffy bounced back and forth in a 'go for it' aerobic display.

"Twenty minutes with our Patented Aerobics Board converts this Pilates Reformer into a complete workout machine. And you're good to go aerobically."

Meredith giggled on the phone.

"Are you telling me," Meredith said. "That she doesn't know that Pilates is anaerobic exercise? So this is a Pilates Fat Burner now."

Before she could answer, a call-in purchaser answered it for them.

"Hi Donna," the woman said. "I love your show. Hi Buffy."

The caller went on to describe in her bouncy voice how she bounced herself to a whopping five pound loss. She now weighed a mere 182 pounds.

"This is awful," Meredith said. "I don't understand it."

But Johanna did. She had read the market research. Fitness equipment home shopping was big business. Women, unhappy with their weight, watched the exercise 'shows', bought the machines, and then moved them from the house to the garage where they kept the extra, fully loaded refrigerator. Did they buy them knowing that then they could call in and rave?

"They're using bungees," she said.

"Bungees?" Meredith asked.

"Long story," Johanna said. "I'll tell you later. Meredith, tell me why I shouldn't come home."

"Hmm," she said. "Let's see. Because Santa Fe is full of fascinating people who share your interests and life philosophy."

"Keep talking," she said.

"Okay," she said. "Because at the end of the day, decent weather is more important than living at the crossroads of the world."

"Nice one."

"I'm not done yet," Meredith insisted. "How about this: because the BodyMind Institute is doing really well and you've got all the support you need there. Should I go on?"

She didn't have to. It wasn't a tough case to make. Watching the on-air bouncing, Johanna made up her mind just as she always did on truly important decisions. Quickly. Unlike the legal establishment and the Pilates community.

"What's the real estate market like these days, Meredith?"

"Insane," she said. "I'll have my broker call you. She got me a deal on a two bedroom on Prince Street. But I don't want a phone call from her in two weeks telling me you're having second thoughts."

"Hello? This is Johanna. The original burn the bridges girl. I'm circling the furniture now figuring out what to take. What's a second thought?"

"Good," she said. "So that's Buffy, huh? She's very

pretty and very persuasive."

Johanna agreed. "She is the home shopper's ulti-mate fantasy. Exercise Barbie."

And the ultimate weapon. Without the exclusivity of the Pilates trademark, Buffy knew that she had to figure out how to still "own" Pilates on TV as now any competitor could use the Pilates name and threaten her TV fran chise. But she did have an ace in the hole: her patented addition. So it had come full circle. The patent trumped the trademark.

Johanna knew that in the professional segment, her market, that with the name liberated and Pilates now the number one trend in fitness, the competition would be huge. Pilates Certification and videos and equipment and memberships and books would be opportunities that would stretch way beyond their inner circle. Just to stay in the game, the Institute's programs would have to be better than the rest. Innovative, cutting edge. Johanna couldn't do this all alone in Santa Fe. She needed to go back to where she had first found Pilates.

New York.

Home.

25

CATHY

"Male athletes get no pain, big gains from Pilates. After years of the no-pain, no-gain school of thought, male professional athletes say they appreciate the kinder, gentler, holistic aspect of Pilates."
—USA Today, 2003

T he Soho office was furnished, the phones lines installed, and   Cathy's fresh-from-Staples wire 'in' basket half filled with news articles, Google research, competitors' workshop schedules and other stuff to discuss with Johanna. Then she got her first phone call of the day.

"BodyMind Institute. How can I help you?" Cathy spoke crisply into the receiver.

"Hi. It's Ruthie Koval. Oh! I hear it snowed in Santa Fe this morning."

Um…

"I was there two winters ago, remember? For the Osteoporosis Workshop? Gosh, it was beautiful. Oh, that incredible smell of burning Pinon in the air and the Plaza glistening with snow in the morning sun. What does it look like right now?"

Cathy Hannan glanced out the window at the corner of Spring and Wooster Streets where a three-day old mound of snowplow excreta had acquired a grey-brown skin and was protruding a dirty gym sock and a Starbucks cup.

"It's beautiful," she continued, "you know the office has moved to New York—same 800 number, though."

"New York?" There was hesitancy in her voice.

"Oh," she said. "I thought I was talking to Lee. Who is this?"

"I'm Cathy," she said. "Cathy Hannan. Is there something I can help you with?"

Martha's studio, their newest training base in Dallas, needed some printed materials, but once she realized Cathy was unqualified to expound on the mystical nature of snowfall in Santa Fe, she became all business.

Thirty seconds later, Johanna called.

"I'm stuck here with the movers," she said. "Where are we on the website?"

Johanna never said 'Hello' or wasted time on protocol. Cathy, a seasoned New Yorker, was never-the-less still surprised with each call.

She clicked on the website window on her new Mac. "I'm looking at the latest version now," she told her. "But we're not live yet. Philip called and needs to know if you want a shopping cart for the site so people can order stuff."

Philip was Johanna's son. His media company was designing the website. Her other son, Ross, was involved in a real estate "start-up" venture. The three of them functioned as if creating a company was not much harder than having a garage sale.

"I need to see the website," she said. "Where's my computer? Has it arrived yet? I need one at home."

Cathy checked the shipping status. "It'll be there tomorrow."

Johanna sighed, frustrated with Apple's inability to deliver her computer the second she required one, or, better yet, the day before. "Look," she said. "I need to think about the shopping cart. What if they order the materials and then we decide they're not qualified to take our course?"

Cathy checked the Stat Pilates website which she'd been

studying all morning. "Doesn't stop the competition," she said. "One click and everything you need is there."

"Yes," Johanna said. "But their courses are all separate. They approach Pilates as if each apparatus was on a different planet. We teach that it's all connected. Look, I can't get into this right now. You're meeting me later at Move Now, right?"

Cathy clicked on her calendar. "Twelve o'clock. 33 Grand Street."

Johanna hung up.

Cathy was still amazed at Johanna's telephone style. For the first two weeks of her employment as the General Manager, her responsibilities took place almost exclusively over the phone or via email. She was sure Johanna didn't like her. Then she realized that she was misreading Johanna's words. Or rather the missing unsaid words. The simple fact was that Johanna's small talk repertoire was extremely limited. She just didn't get conversational formalities. If she did ask how you were, she expected specifics. If someone tossed her a 'Have a nice day' Johanna could just as easily expound on why that wouldn't be possible on that specific Wednesday due to a dental appointment, or say nothing. 'How's it going?' was open ended enough to be downright scary. After 12 years in the advertising industry, where every smile might be calculated and every word laden with contradictory subtext, Cathy found that Johanna's bluntness was actually refreshing once you realized it had nothing to do with you personally. It's not that Johanna didn't have the time to talk. She could spend 15 minutes describing how much someone had eaten in a Japanese restaurant and why ethnic foods hadn't improved the American palate. She just didn't understand the point of conversation that lacked real content or controversy.

Before Johanna hired her, Cathy was hardly a fitness expert. She'd heard of Pilates, looked at the splashy layouts in *Fitness* magazine on the subway home, and hadn't Madonna even sung about it in one of her songs? But it wasn't just Pilates that attracted her to the job. She had tired of 'focus groups.' She found their explanations of which colors they perceived as more 'suburban' mighty tedious. Advertising stuff that Americans didn't need, couldn't afford, and probably didn't even want, had become too hard to dismiss as she took the elevator down each night. This Pilates business seemed, by comparison, non-evil. Plus, she wanted a job less compartmentalized. Cathy wasn't an expert in marketing, PR, or management, but knew she could move about in all three.

For her part, Johanna was more suspicious than impressed with experts. She didn't need corporate relocation specialists or executive recruiters. Her approach to business required the knack to grab hold. New skills. Fast/Now.

Neither did she interview dozens of candidates to hire the right people. And, she had been right about Cathy. She had closed up the Santa Fe operation and moved it 2000 miles. Their computers and phones shut down at 5:00pm Mountain time on a Monday and were operational on Tuesday at 8:00am Eastern time. Not one order or membership or course registration was delayed. The plan worked without a blip. Johanna had commented, "Even Napoleon couldn't have planned or executed such a flawless campaign."

Now, after only a few weeks, they were totally settled, and Cathy wanted to learn about how the Institute training program really differed from the competition she had been checking out. She was pleased that Johanna asked her to see it in action at their New York training base, Move Now.

They met at 12:30 in the entryway of Move Now. The bulletin board by the front door was crammed with at least thirty flyers for massage therapists, private yoga sessions, Reiki healers, guitar lessons, back support lumbar cushions, all that you'd expect. But the biggest flyer listed the studio's own workshop schedule.

"Gyro workshop. Ball Rolling Workshop. Yoga. I thought this was our Pilates Certifying Studio," Cathy said.

Johanna studied the schedule. "Unbelievable. We advertise for them, send them bodies for Pilates workshops and then they turn around and hustle them for their own workshops. I should send them a bill for our percentage."

"In Vegas if you're caught hustling they'd cut you off literally. Why don't you stop this?" she said.

"Later. I am pacing myself in the process of learning patience. They say it comes from the inside out. How am I doing on the out part?" Johanna laughed as she led Cathy through the tiny reception area, past the curtained-off changing rooms and into the studio proper where Susie Schultz was putting eight clients through a Reformer class.

"Hmm," Cathy said.

"What?"

"I didn't know they taught group Reformer classes. I thought it was all one-on-one."

"We started them," Johanna said. "Seven years ago. Re-choreographed the exercises so that you do supine, then kneeling. Joe's original exercise order meant that you were always changing position which won't work with a group. This makes for a smoother class."

In the studio, all eight women lay on their backs while revolving their legs in wide circles.

"No men?" Cathy observed.

Johanna nodded. "Too gynecological-looking."

"Yeah. Men don't do the missionary position in public." Cathy was enjoying the easy repartee between them.

"Men are a challenge in many ways. When it comes to Pilates, they lack flexibility and since they want bulky muscles, we're a hard sell. But you can get taller wih Pilates. Maybe that will get them on their backs!" Cathy nodded. "There's no shortage of 'bulk' in this group. I thought everyone would be thin."

"Dream on," Johanna answered. "This here is real time. When I started doing Pilates, in the dark ages as my kids describe it, there were only skinny people. We wore pastel leotards and no tights. Believe it."

Glancing across the line up of sweatpants and over-sized t-shirts, Cathy didn't want to imagine it. She pointed to the little wooden apparatus in the corner, which she'd learned from her Pilates cramming was called the Wunda Chair. "Only one of those?" she asked.

"Nobody uses it," Johanna said. "They don't even know the exercises. I have redesigned this box on paper, but I haven't found someone to work with me on prototypes."

"Too bad, you could fit three of them for any one Reformer in the same real estate."

"You catch on fast. Remember when talking to Pilates teachers that they prefer a slower pace, not fast forward, more like slow and stopped."

At the end of the class, Suzie came over to introduce herself and invite them to watch a teacher training lecture that was about to begin.

"Listen," Johanna whispered. "Our program is based on teaching Pilates a la Socrates. Our competition teaches by performing or pontificating."

Cathy nodded and summoned up her freshman Intro to Philosophy class.

"We want our teachers to help these students to conceptualize as they are moving," Johanna said. "Asking them questions, finding out what they know and understand, rather than just demo-ing or talking too much."

A ha. Socrates. Right.

"This is a common problem," Johanna said. "These Pilates teachers come from dance backgrounds where their teachers were God and sometimes they assume this role when they begin to teach."

"And the students?" Cathy asked. "Who are they?"

"This group are former dancers," she said. "But it is changing. We are getting physical therapists, yoga teachers, personal trainers. They will challenge these teachers, not just meekly absorb. They won't be sitting there mute while someone drones on about articulation."

After watching for half an hour more, they left, picked up a couple of sandwiches and headed back to the office.

"Nice light in our office. Not Santa Fe, but better than I remembered," Johanna said around a mouthful of her chicken salad sandwich.

"We'll have your office set up by the end of the week," Cathy continued. "The bookcase will be here tomorrow. You know, I was thinking about Suzie and the students. Well, here we are training people on all this equipment, but not selling any of it." Cathy pulled out an elegant and very professional looking brochure from the Stat Pilates Company and set it on the desk. "Look at that," she said. "Vertically integrated—pardon the management speak. When you take a teacher training course with them, you learn on their equipment. It's total Pilates."

" True," Johanna said. "Our Certifying Studios use Kent's equipment primarily but they also have Stat and Prism apparatus."

"And the Chair?" Cathy said. "Why don't we do a deal with one of them on your redesigned Chair?"

"Because they're all competing with us. Pilates is a religion now and they have their own churches. What I can't understand is why they are also supporting this new Association for the Pilates Method which is going to be like the Vatican. The last thing any of us needs is a Pope, especially one that is supposed to be infallible."

Johanna pointed to a gift-wrapped box on the file cabinet. "What's that?"

"Oh yeah." She handed it to her. "Christmas present from Bodyworks Studio."

She put down her sandwich and peeled the studiously non-religious but vaguely seasonal wrapping paper away. From her ad days, Cathy knew what this time of the year meant. Piles of fruit baskets, popcorn tins, smoked salmon, artsy little soaps and other 'please-keep-hiring-us' tokens.

Johanna pulled out an expensive candle and sniffed it.

"I guess these will start rolling in now."

Johanna laughed. "You know how many we received last year? Three."

"Really?" she said. She already had been mentally distributing candles around the apartment she shared with her boyfriend.

"I can't explain this without a major diatribe about New Age platitudes about spirituality and living in the present, and all the other phony shit that interferes with getting the job done. Americans used to be fearless and straight talking. Now they are a bunch of wimps. What does this have to do with the gift question. Nothing and everything. Stay tuned and in time it will make sense. I told you that this would end with a diatribe. Make you wish you were back at the ad agency?" she asked.

"Aubergine is this year's plum. Noir might be next Fall's midnight." Cathy mimicked. "No thanks. We've got personality issues here, but it is still relatively benign. But we need our own Pilates machine and that's why we should do the Chair," Cathy said. "I'm game to get it going."

"Maybe I can talk to Prism. Julie London who runs it is fairly new to this business. She doesn't have the psychological baggage we old timers can't escape. Her Pilates equipment manufacturing company is the smallest of the three, but she gaining on the other two now that the trademark is history. She is beautiful, bright and ambitious. Let's get a prototype of my design and then I will call her."

In her old job, Cathy wouldn't have been so bold as to toss around business ideas over sandwiches with the boss, who would have later claimed them as her own. But she knew that she didn't have to be cautious in this one. Cathy clicked onto Explorer and started a search for a mechanical engineer who just might have heard of Pilates.

26

NEW YORK

"A 2003 survey of nearly 3000 New York elementary school children found that 24 percent were obese and 19 percent overweight."
—The **New York Times**, 2006

Johanna looked at the box of Pinon-scented incense that Lee had sent her as a holiday gift. Included also was a Christmas card that had been mailed to their former Palace Street address. Postmarked Paris, it read: *Chère Johanna, Joyeux Noël, Bisoux, Guy.* Looking at these tokens from her former life, Johanna had to admit she missed these friends. And she also had to put these thoughts behind her now. She was starting over again, albeit in a New York that had changed a lot in these past 12 years.

Johanna turned and looked at herself in the mirror assessing the damage from years of nonstop stress. She still had the look of a quintessential New Yorker, but she knew she was due for an upgrade. Her sons had told her she was not too old to pull it off. "Our old neighborhood is so over, Mom," they had said. "Nothing uptown, puleez." Forget that in her last re-incarnation as an uptown New Yorker she had never gone south of 42nd Street except for occasional jazz at the Village Gate. But things had really changed. She noticed the dress codes first. Even on Park Avenue anything was okay in today's no rules environment. Maybe they were tourists, but underwear as outerwear, running gear adorning bodies that hadn't moved in decades, shoes that were once slippers, and, the most objectionable, the garish thong pulled a bit too high over jeans that were pushed a bit too low forcing the eye into a vortex of the unsightly.

Better to forget that part, that New York of yesterday, which epitomized elegance and sophistication. Today was the dawn of the New York minute. Soho, Tribeca, the East Village were its standard bearers. The standard was hip and Johanna was ready to play along and reinvent herself once again. Santa Fe had tested her, undoubtedly, but it hadn't dulled her spark or depleted her energy.

Once she had settled into her new 'downtown' apartment, Meredith suggested meeting for lunch. Johanna emerged from the sidewalk throng on Prince Street looking confident and hip wrapped in a "classic" camel coat made au courant in sheared mink rather than cloth. "Welcome back." A siren's blare interrupted Meredith as it dopplered down Broadway.

"Thanks for your tip on neighborhoods. I really like it here in Hip Central, but it can get expensive," Johanna replied."

"Yesterday I went out for a slice of pizza and came back with a $900 Hogan bag. Fortunately it was on sale, so I took it off their hands for a mere $600."

Meredith laughed and steered her past the Vuitton store on their way to Zoë.

They went inside and a stiletto-heeled young hostess seated them at a table in the back. It was one o'clock and Zoë was packed with the usual downtown business crowd: publicists, movie producers, agents, photographers, the odd vaguely recognizable actor. As they wove between the tables, several glances confirmed that they were still it girls.

"You look great, Meredith," Johanna said once they were seated. "When did you decide to go short with your hair? I like it. And you've lightened it."

Meredith raked her fingers through her chiseled locks. "It's fun, but I'm in the salon every six weeks. So tell me. How's Cathy working out? She seems smart."

"Great," she said. "Perfect. She knows how to take charge. And there's no tip toeing around her. She understands that we call it work because you get paid to do it. Tell me what you've been up to. But first tell me what to order. What's good here?"

"Look at that." Meredith pointed to a waiter carrying two huge plates with enormous burgers and mounds of fries.

"Who would have guessed we would reach the point of the one pound burger," she said.

Johanna laughed, glancing around the restaurant. "Strange," she said. "I had hoped New York was immune to food as your best friend. Airports are the worst. The smells, the containers, people eating right off their laps everywhere you are."

Meredith shook her head. "Grande portions followed the Nouvelle Cuisine experiment. What my parents once called chargers, the decorative place plates, are now becoming the standard plate size. Remember salad plates? It seems a lifetime ago. Sorry. I'm preaching."

"Go ahead," Johanna said. "Saves me from doing it. I've been gone too long. I swear right here in Gotham the population has grown fatter. And the young, less time on the planet, but even they are fat. Are we all in a race. Has life become one big watermelon-eating contest? Meredith order something for us I have gone and lost my appetite."

Meredith looked at the menu. "You're not doing Atkins or anything, right?"

Johanna put down her menu and dead-panned,

"Meredith for Christ's sake. I was in Santa Fe not abducted by aliens. I'll eat anything that has taste. You decide though, you're the nutritionist to the beautiful."

When the waiter returned, Meredith ordered two cocktails, a Martini and a Campari and soda for Johanna, but then informed the waiter that they would split an endive and goat cheese salad and one pasta primavera.

"The funny thing," Meredith said "All the modeling agencies are downtown. The restaurants are packed with size two women, but you can't get anything but a size sixteen meal. And the staff can be so intimidating if you order an appetizer or ask to share. Did you see our waiter's look?"

Johanna laughed. "Do you remember early Nouvelle Cuisine? Six foot business men would be served three tiny vegetables rolling about on gleaming white plates."

"Well, we've sure swung back. Way back."

Glancing around the restaurant, Meredith explained that the situation was serious. "You know," she said. "Professionally, I'm treating obese children."

The waiter returned with the salad and an extra plate. Dividing the salad, Meredith explained portion overload, "This appetizer is about ten bites for each of us. You know

I've been counting bites in order to identify correct portions. This is supposed to be an appetizer and it's entrée sized. You know why?"

"Go ahead."

"God, I'm boring you."

"Meredith, please" she said. "When I'm bored, I'll let you know. Like everyone else I'm a bit of a closet crazy. What makes people angry interests me."

"Right," Meredith said. "First of all, this salad is huge because nobody drinks any more. Restaurants used to make most of their money on alcohol," she said. "With everybody sober we've got to pay for this table on the expansion plan. Look around."

Johanna nodded.

"With the loss of liquor profits everyone scrambled to increase portions and dress it up by throwing in a few porcini mushrooms here and there. This salad cost the restaurant a couple of bucks at most. Did you see it on the menu? It's $ 19?"

"I was seeing you take more of the goat cheese."

"The thing is, it was originated by the Nixon

administration."

Johanna had a sip of her drink as she struggled to tease out the connection. "That damn cloth coat." she said.

"I'm telling you, nobody wants to hear this. Nixon was unpopular, so his Secretary of Agriculture, Earl Butz, suggested the way back to the hearts and minds of America was through their bellies. Farm subsidies leading to cheap food. We became the richest nation with the cheapest food. In Africa, with plenty of arable land, they can't afford to compete with our agricultural production costs. The point is, with food this cheap, the market's response has been increased portion size. So here we are."

The waiter brought their lone entrée but couldn't resist bristling when asked for a second plate.

"So how's your press these days?" Johanna said. "I haven't seen your name as much. You still doing interviews?"

"All they want is a sound bite about how pine nuts are the new super food. I refuse to do it."

"Super foods," Johanna said. "I think *Time* Magazine had a cover story about that."

"Don't remind me," Meredith said. "My grandfather

would die all over again if he knew what his magazine was publishing. It's crazy. Don't eat white foods. Don't eat rice. One third of the world lives on rice—the skinny third of the world, by the way—and we're supposed to believe it makes us fat."

"Blueberries," Johanna said. "I think that was one of the super foods."

Meredith nodded. "Blueberries, lentils, broccoli. Not pasta. How do you like the pasta?"

"Nice," Johanna said. "I remember being in our local organic market right after that article and all I could think about were blueberries. Who doesn't want to be smarter? No need to study. Eat the blue and increase your IQ. Snappy, right? The Department of Commerce in Maine should hire me. But how come everyone in Maine isn't a genius?"

"There's no logic and remember this, no humor. But lots of conversation. That's one of the many reasons why this is so out of control. Americans aren't interested in trade deficits or global warming, but the subject of eating is always ripe. Everyone eats so the media can always fill up on food stories."

"You know, Meredith," Johanna said. "Why can't you get the word out?"

"Less and less possible. Magazines don't want an article on moderation and portion control. Too boring and you can't wrap an ad campaign around it. Nothing to sell, no advertisers. The entire country went on Atkins, editors included. A 30 year old diet that was rejected because it was unhealthy became the new gospel. Dieting fads have a long prosperous history in America."

"I'm still listening and buying lunch by the way, so don't argue." Johanna reached into her wallet to retrieve a credit card.

"Thanks, and next time it's on me," Meredith said. "So let's go back to the sixties. Back then if you wanted to lose weight, you just ate fewer calories."

"No, thank you," Johanna said too loudly. "I'm not teasing my hair again. Remember those girdles? Forget it."

At the table next to them, a woman glanced up from her Pellegrino at Johanna's sudden outburst.

"Excuse me I couldn't help over hearing your con- versation. Personally, I'm nostalgic for the seventies when fat made us fat. What happened there? That was a lot easier to keep up with. Fat free? Fat-free sounded patriotic."

"What happened was the flavor was liberated as

well," Meredith said. Fat delivers flavor and fullness. Cutting down on fat does make sense if you are just thinking calories. There are nine calories per fat gram. Protein and carbohydrates have four calories per gram. But if you don't feel full and then you eat twice as much, well you see where we are going..."said Meredith.

"A friend's daughter," the woman said. "Mid-seventies. She'd been obsessing about her weight since she was a teenager, and she was ecstatic because pasta became the new must eat, low fat food, without the alfredo sauce, of course."

"Early eighties. Enter Atkins," Meredith continued. "Who says there are no second acts? Second time around his timing was perfect because fat free meant sugar added. Remember cooler shelves of fat free yogurts or Snackwell, the famous low fat cookies? The manufacturers doubled the amount of sugar to compensate for the fat loss. Next we have a nation of sugar addicts."

"Sorry ladies I've got to go, but please save us all! Whenever you figure it out, send me a case." She handed Johanna her business card, said goodbye and left.

"I'm ending here too." Meredith commented. Sixty-eight percent of Americans are overweight/ obese. And it's only getting worse. Let's take a walk and get away from food. It's not too cold out, is it?"

Johanna finished signing the credit card slip. "Sounds great. We can go shopping. It's the American way. Eating or buying merchandise. Guess I need some boots for the new Hogan bag."

Outside, Soho was bustling with the usual lunch hour crowd, plus an extra dose of office escapees enjoying the infrequent December sunshine.

"Let's head into Nolita," Johanna said. "I've heard the shops are trendier and the prices easier." They stopped to browse the window in Sigerson Morrison. Meredith pointed out a pair of brown leather wedge-heel boots.

"Nice," Johanna said. "Maybe I'll try them on later. I'd rather go to the store you've been raving about while I've been in exile in Santa Fe."

They kept walking until they reached Meredith's favorite boutique, Language.

Inside where architecture books mingled with luscious cashmeres draped over a Harley Davidson motorcycle, they fingered the buttery leather jackets under the watchful eye of the salesgirl, who Johanna couldn't help noticing wore a tight fitting tank top that terminated just above the protruding flab of her belly. She was about twenty pounds over her fighting weight, which she could have easily camouflaged with the latest baggy tunic, but instead she highlighted the shape with a pair of tight-fitting low-riding jeans and a cropped top. Johanna looked up and noticed that Meredith had picked up on the salesgirl's garb. After some more browsing, they left and continued back to Johanna's office.

Outside, the sun dipped behind some clouds and the afternoon grew cold.

"It's funny," Johanna said, as they strolled back towards Broadway. "When we were that age, you'd never find an overweight sales girl at a stylish boutique. You'd be lucky if they sold anything beyond a size six."

"It's all changed. People come to me who are thirty pounds overweight and you know what they say?"

"Can I lose weight and eat eight times a day?" Johanna answered.

"No. They say they just want to 'eat healthy.' They won't even admit they're overweight. Of course, they're seeing me to lose weight. But they can't come out and say it."

When they got to the entrance of her building, Johanna stopped, looked at Meredith and said, "Do you have time to come upstairs? I found this interactive diet site

I want to show you."

"OK, but just to see the office. There's nothing but hype in diets. Trust me. Last week I got an email about a "Slimming Soap." Just shower and get skinny. Wash the fat away. They are probably selling millions of cases of the stuff. Since practically no one is thin, do their customers think that only they can buy this magic soap?"

Upstairs in Johanna's office, Meredith looked over the site. She was totally unimpressed with its content, as Johanna knew she would be. It wasn't, however, what they were selling but how—the vehicle—that she wanted to sell her on. Johanna had been thinking that Meredith's low quantity diet was really new and could work in this interactive format. She broached the subject of a partnership.

"Why? No one wants to eat this way. We'd be wasting our time and money."

"No one wanted Pilates either, and now it is the biggest trend in fitness."

"And look where it got you being first. You lost money and you almost lost your health. Why don't we let someone else stick his or her neck out?"

"But this is your concept. America has dieted with

low calorie, low fat, and low carb. There is nothing else left but low quantity."

"Maybe, but it is probably too late, too. And, if it took off, then everyone would just copy it."

"No they wouldn't. This time around I'd make certain that we had it all locked up. Trademarks, copyrights, and maybe even patents. Perhaps a product. A device that would count bites. At least people couldn't delude themselves about how much they are actually eating. Just this awareness would make a difference."

"I have to admit I would hate to wake up and read in the *Post* that someone else had a best-selling book based on my low quantity diet."

"Good. So we are good to go, as they say on TV shopping. We'd have to get on TV."

"And here I thought that we were just friends getting together for lunch."

"Friends and business partners," Johanna said. She liked the sound of it.

27

MARTA

"Pilates, an exercise method involving controlled, non-impact movements that engage both body and mind has today become part of the fitness industry's lexicon. Because of the media attention, many fitness facilities have found little or no need to advertise it."
—IDEA Health & Fitness Source, 2001

"I am so sick of hearing that Pilates is all about the core," Johanna announced one day. "Did we think up that phrase? It's such an oversimplification, so yesterday. Today's body issues need to be addressed differently. Cathy, how are you at tweaking?"

"Pilates been successfully branded, why confuse things with something else?" Cathy countered.

A year and a half into her tenure at the Institute, and Cathy had finally figured out the driving force behind Johanna: the need for Change, as Mabel Dodge Luhan called it with a capital C. And even though she publicly agreed that 'if it's not broken don't fix it,' Cathy knew Johanna never accepted that old saw.

Johanna always referred to herself as the 'the dumbest

smart person alive.' She was a bit clueless about how body people 'processed.' What did that modern idiom mean, 'processing?' Johanna herself was keen on thinking or moving or moving and thinking, and felt that processing was to thinking what dieting was to eating. She could not comprehend why thinking had been replaced by processing somewhere in the mid-eighties and why it was particularly popular with body people. It felt to her like a recessive gene gone haywire. Whenever she tried to talk about the business of the body business, she was keenly aware that the world she inhabited was not looking toward the future, but was slowly processing the now. A subtle difference, but one that caused her great agitation. Cathy was beginning to recognize the dynamic and to step in when Johanna began to lose her limited patience skills.

Despite Cathy's admonition that Pilates and core were almost synonymous, Johanna, who always lived in the future, saw that the core focus was not going to be adequate for a graying America. Which is why on a warm spring afternoon, they were heading uptown in an over-air-conditioned cab to see Marta Miller at her Dance Physical Therapy Clinic opposite Lincoln Center. Miller, a Physical Therapist, Doctor of Oriental Medicine, President of the Dance Medicine Foundation, and Pilates expert, had the expertise that Johanna knew was needed if Pilates was going to maintain its position.

"In our newest evolution, the Pilates Method will need to be more than tweaked—we'll need the big guns. Real knowledge," explained Johanna.

"You've mentioned Marta Miller's advice before. What's up now? She and her staff are responsible for keeping the entire City Ballet on their toes, right?" said Cathy.

"She's the one. But dancers represent less than one tenth of one percent of the world population. There are only another 6 billion who need her brilliance. That's what we're going to propose. We need her help."

They arrived at Dance Physical Therapy at six pm, just as Marta was finishing up with her client, a City Ballet dancer with limbs of inhumanly long length, perhaps nineteen years old or so, whose exquisite knee appeared to be out of sorts. Six other therapists were working on limbs of the celebrated or talented who also suffered various pains from performing. Several gorgeous specimens draped themselves over Pilates apparatus conditioning themselves against injury. Every therapist and dancer, whether in sweats or leotards, leg warmers and artfully torn T-shirts, revealed bodies too perfect to ignore. Although the studio was a plain, no-nonsense affair, visual excitement vibrated. Cathy, who discreetly blended in with her minimalist black attire, commented that it felt like being inside a living anatomy lab. Everybody in the room was part of this tableau vivant, except for Johanna. Dressed in a Ralph Lauren navy pin stripped jacket and skinny pants in a Euro blue black hue, Jimmy Choo sling back stilettos and Marni cropped black silk sweater, Johanna stood confidently in front of a full length mirror and pushed her auburn French twist gently up a notch off her nape, securing it with a silver comb. Cathy smiled knowingly. Johanna had calculated every detail. If the crowd was casual, Johanna was done up. If she thinks important clothes are *de rigueur*, she's in Diesel. Never fall below the radar screen in the appearance department she'd explained to Cathy more than once.

Marta, straddling a wooden stool at the end of a massage table, looked up from her young client whose calloused feet she was now holding in her magical hands and caught Johanna's eye. She mouthed "one minute".

"You'll like Marta," Johanna said quietly while they waited.   "She's Hungarian, like me. Came here as a child, right after the Revolution."

"Cool," Cathy responded.

Marta had an unmistakable European look, as did several of the dancers, who were surely recruits from the best foreign troupes. When Marta joined them, she led the way to a private acupuncture room in a separate wing of her clinic. They moved three chairs inside to have a proper sit down meeting.

"Cathy right?" Marta asked.

"Why yes, hello."

They shook hands and Marta sat on one of the chairs behind the padded massage table, which filled up most of the space. Against the clinical décor, Johanna looked even more dramatic.

"You look good," Marta said to Johanna. "Not surprisingly, I knew you as one to take good care of yourself. How's it to be back, from...?"

"Out there, and never again. I've ordered the staff to shoot me with one of those tranquilizer guns the game and wild life folks use if I ever get confused again. She pushed one of the chairs forward. "Rest, Cathy."

Johanna rejected the other chair, choosing to lean against one of the massage tables with ankles crossed. "It's nice to be here among these beautiful bodies," she said.

Marta nodded. "It doesn't often look like reality here, on the surface, that is, but the problems we experience are actually not dissimilar from the general population."

"Such as?" Cathy asked.

"Lots of stress fractures." Marta said

"From overwork?" asked Johanna

Marta shook her head. "No, Osteoporosis."

"In dancers? I thought that was an older woman's disease," Cathy said genuinely surprised.

"And a disease of malnutrition," Marta answered soberly.

"From Anorexia?" Johanna continued.

"No, no," Marika said. "Anorexia isn't that common in dancers. That's a myth. No, what I'm talking about is basic malnutrition. American foods come off manufacturing lines in plastic. They are nutritionally deficient. What most teenagers live on. During the years when they should be laying down bone material for life, they're grazing in food courts at their local mall. Needless to say, they're not getting what they need."

"It's hard to think about malnutrition when by 2010 the prediction is that half of our kids will be overweight or even obese. I know this sounds impossible, but I edited a speech that Meredith is giving next week and the statistics are scary. Now you tell us that there

is osteoporosis in the young from eating nutrient deficient foods. And we have Type 2 diabetes from eating
too much of these foods," said Johanna. "Can't
Americans find some other way to entertain themselves
other than eating?"

"What these trends forecast is that those who believe
Pilates is only for healthy bodies will find themselves with
empty Reformers," Marta observed.

"So," Johanna says. "First, we had everybody running and jumping and doing high impact aerobics and ending up with injuries."

"Right," Marta said slowly, as if waiting for the connection to become evident to Cathy.

"Then people moved into Pilates which was less
stressful for joints since most of the exercises are performed
lying down," Cathy postulated.

"Uh-huh," Marta said.

"So," Johanna said. "Between the population of mal-
nourished young people and the huge population of seniors
who aren't aging so gracefully, we have a problem that we
didn't anticipate. Both ends of the demographic spectrum
are at risk for osteoporosis.

"And then add that people now spend most of their time sitting in flexion with their legs crossed."

"So where do we stand, right now, today, at 7 pm. ?"

Marta swiveled slowly in her chair. "I believe the key today is weight-bearing exercise. It stresses the muscles, which puts stress on the bones."

"This is good?" Cathy asked, unsure.

"Absolutely," Marta said. "The bones respond to the stress by rebuilding, what we call remodeling. As we age, remodeling slows down. We need to stimulate it."

"With weight-bearing exercise." Johanna asserted, looking over at Cathy with "the look" she knew meant: file this.

"Yes," Marta continues. "All the sedentary people among us. Not moving, not walking, but sitting all day, adaptively shortening their joints to one position without even knowing the ill effects."

"What do you mean by adaptively shorten?" Cathy asked, reflectively turning to Johanna.

"To really over-simplify, when one sits too long

muscles don't get any information, they have nothing to respond to, so they lose their responsiveness. Atrophy sets in."

"Plus," Marta continues, "Weight bearing, strangely enough, stimulates the inner ear which as we all know controls balance."

"You don't fall and break your hip," Johanna says.

Marta nodded. "By the way, when is the new Chair going to be ready?

Johanna's face lit up. "The Chair. It's good isn't it?" she says.

"I love the Chair," she said. "Many weight bearing exercises and some excellent rotational movements too."

"Somehow, we need to incorporate weight-bearing into the matwork. Get people on their feet," Johanna said.

"Kind of defeats the purpose of the mat," Cathy, sensing she had made a faux pas, then added "Doesn't it?"

Marta shrugged. "Look, 50 percent of the population shouldn't be doing some of these exercises because of disc issues. And a lot of them don't know it. But the moves are in the current Pilates videos, which anyone can buy and do at home."

Johanna looked up suddenly. "Look," she said, "The population has changed. We're not the same profile as in the forties when Joe developed this for a small elite clientele."

"We've been working on advancing things, Marta. Cathy knows I've been studying the Chair for ages. We know the demographics. The aging of the population. Obesity. What you have told us today means we have to find new solutions. Let's get clients off their backs and reduce forward flexion in our supine exercises. Standing, weight bearing, more extension exercises, more lateral bending and rotational movements. We have to do it so that Pilates remains the best exercise."

Johanna laughed then started pacing again. "Cathy, look I'm processing!"

"What would Joe say?" Cathy asked.

Marta's eyes drifted to the ceiling as she considered the question. "He'd say 'What's next? What do people need'?"

"Then let's get moving," said Johanna. "We can't keep Joe waiting."

28

MEREDITH'S SPEECH

"Why do researchers insist on investigation of obesity as if it were a subject for the X-Files? Too much emphasis is placed on obesity as a disease... Instead of pinning our hopes on finding the chemical factor... we should be looking at how Americans' eating habits have changed in the past 50 years."
—**Meredith Luce,** *Time* **Magazine Letters, 2002**

The following speech was given by Meredith Luce MS, RD, LN to the Society of Bariatric Physicians June 2005

The Size of America

In 2030, just 25 years from now, almost everyone in American will be super-sized. Projections indicate that almost all of the adult population will be overweight or obese. My name is Meredith Luce and I am a Nutrition Professional, one of those experts responsible for educating America about food groups and nutrients. I am here today to question this mission for the obvious reason: our failure to make a difference. We are now in the midst of an obesity epidemic that, despite our efforts at education, continues to grow.

Today, right now, the US population, 285 million, has 130 million overweight, obese and morbidly obese adults. That's almost 7 out of 10 of us. Seventy percent of the population is too big. This means that if you are in a room with ten people, it is possible that seven of the bodies will be fat. If you are in a room with ten people and none of them is fat, you are probably in the fashion division of the Ford Modeling Agency or on the stage of the New York City Ballet.

To find out why this happened, I analyzed the data going back almost 50 years to 1958, when we consumed 1900 calories daily and obesity was almost nonexistent. Today our nation produces 3800 calories per person. Using USDA "spoilage" factor of 1100 calories, the official estimate of consumption is "only" 2700 calories per adult person. In my opinion, given the current technology, spoilage is probably less. If so, an estimate of a daily 3000 calories consumed may be more accurate. But with either figure, 2700 or 3000 calories, it is obvious that we eat too much, too often. So different from the 1950s when:

1. People ate meals and only meals sitting together as families. Typically 3 meals a day and no snacks other than for small children who needed additional nutritional input. To grow vertically, let's remember!

2. Adults were more active on a daily basis perhaps because they had to push a lawnmower or get up to adjust the antenna on the TV. Still, sitting was the preferred position, then and now. Now, in front of a computer; then to play cards and board games; to listen to the radio; to write letters; to read books.

3. Almost 50 percent of adults smoked cigarettes. A *New York Times* article, *"They Replaced Cigarettes with Bagels"* (12/19/03) by Gina Kolata explains that this shift also led to increased consumption, because 'eating healthy' came to mean that if it were good for you, then more of it is better still.

4. The dinner plate was ten inches in total, but the eating surface was only seven inches, compared to twelve inches today.

Here's what was NOT happening in the 1950's:
• Working out wasn't even a concept; health clubs didn't exist.
• No one had even heard of a carb.
• No one had any idea about good/bad fats.
• There were no diet sodas or diet foods.
• Snacking, now called grazing, was infrequent.

Between 1965-1975, the U.S. Government, the U.S. Agricultural industry, the food companies, the bottled water business, health clubs, publishers, and the new diet businesses hit upon the mantra that has been their signature ever since: Eat Healthy and Exercise More. Obviously exercise services and bottled water. The public was led to believe that excess consumption could be handled by beating it off and flushing it out. Today sales of these businesses are estimated to be about one and a half trillion dollars, making them crucial to our 13 trillion GNP.

This absolute acceptance of the 'Eat Healthy, Exercise More' mantra means that the food, fitness, and water industries needn't apologize for the size of the American waistband. And because of a huge cultural change that has occurred in the past decade, no individual who is fat has to feel apologetic, either. Americans have the right—it is our blessed way of life, to quote our President—to over consume and to have our bodies accommodated, which, luckily, provides new commercial opportunities. These include enlargement of clothing, transport, and furniture for home, hotel, hospital, school, theatre, and stadium. These developments have been widely reported, beginning with seat belt extensions, SUVs, king-sized coffins, followed by bigger seats everywhere. Even as far away as London, theatre owners fear they are losing ticket sales because they can't accommodate the American 'seat'.

In the apparel area, there is total acceptance and assistance. Twenty years ago, fat men had to go to the 'Husky Department' which had a limited selection while women bought maternity tops or muu-muus. Now manufacturers accommodate in two ways. One, re-sizing so that

today's 8 is really a 10, and so forth. The second is the avail-
ability of fashionable PLUS sizes. Females can purchase anything from low-rider jeans to camisole tops. The apparel
adaptations have further facilitated total dismemberment of
'appropriate' attire. Since we now have effectively only one
style—casual—being fat is no longer a fashion disadvantage.
For kids it is even easier to fit in if they are fat. Their music
idols are often oversized themselves, or, if not, they espouse
'bagged out' clothing several sizes too big.

*Obviously the economic benefits of developing a new,
super-sized population has given business an opportunity to
reshape almost everything we need for living and dying.*

I opened this speech by stating that in 2030 most
Americans would essentially exist in one size: super. Is this
just hyperbole or are there projections that substantiate this
assertion? Unfortunately, there are statistical analyses that
confirm that 89% of the adult population will be large. Our
2030 population of 363.58 million will comprise 279.24
million adults of whom 248.25 million will be:

Overweight: BMI in the 25-30 range = **99.83** mil (35.75%)
Obese: BMI in the 30-40 range = **126.58** mil (45.33%)
Very Obese: BMI in the 40+ range = **21.84** mil (7.82%)

Now if we look at the historical data from 25 years
ago, 1980, we see that we were well on our way towards

universal bigness.

In 1980, our total population was 225.23 million comprised of 163.54 million adults of whom 80.78 million were:

Overweight: BMI in the 25-30 range = **52.33** mil (32.0%)
Obese: BMI in the 30-40 range = **23.71** mil (23.71%)
Very Obese: BMI in the 40+ range = **4.74** mil (2.9%)

However, in 1980 weight issues were confined to the adult population. Only 6% of children (0-17) were overweight, a total of 3.821 million. But if we look ahead to 2030, we see another picture. The prediction is that 35.0 million children of the total estimated 84.34 million, or 41.5 %, will be overweight/obese. Thus, 88.9% of the adults and 41.5% of the children in the USA will be at risk for chronic disease. If we combine these numbers with the 72 million seniors who will comprise almost 20% of our population, we can envision a nation where almost everyone is sick or old or both.

Given these demographic projections, it is no surprise that a Princeton University economist has estimated that in 2030 health care spending will represent fully 25 percent of our GNP. But, surprisingly, there are economists who believe that this huge health care expenditure will not be unfavorable for our economy. It will just be a redistribution of spending. As a dietician who counsels diabetics daily, I find it hard to accept that spending income on dialysis is no different economically speaking than spending on a vacation.

When I received my degree as a Registered Dietician 25 years ago, I fully expected that my job might become obsolete if my mission and that of my profession—educating the public about nutrition—was successful. I was wrong, but I am not sure that my profession is not functionally obsolete anyway. As I look at the size of America, it occurs to me that it is time to hand this mission over to another profession, that of economics. Because unless economists can figure out how to increase the price of food without impacting our economy, nutritional information will go unheard. Thank you for you attention.

Statistics complied by S. Sonia Gugga, PhD

Sources:

http://www.obesity.org/subs/childhood/prevalence.shtml

Demographics 1998;101;497-504 Pediatrics Richard P. Troiano and Katherine M. Flegal

http://ihcrp.georgetown.edu/agingsociety/pdfs/chronic.pdf

http://www.cdc.gov/mmwr/preview/mmwrhtml/mm5206a2.htm

United Nations Dept of Economic and Social Affairs. World Population in 2300

Future Longevity—Demographic Concerns and Consequences

Kevin G. Kinsella, MA Journal of the American Geriatrics Society

Volume 53 Page S299 - September 2005

http://www.census.gov/population/www/documentation/twps0029/twps0029.html

29

COSMIC BALANCE

"Fat America:....the fastest growing consumer segment. To entrepreneurs, it's a market of potentially immense proportions."

—CNN Money, 2006

Johanna was in her office scrolling through the morning's email assault: meet high quality singles, Hoodia secret weight loss herb (which immediately went into her inbox) interest-free mortgages, and several dozen others too vulgar to read in the daylight, when she got a phone call from Jerome Steinberg.

"Hi Johanna," he said. "You probably don't remember me."

Wrong. She remembered him. They had met leaving the office of Dick Shelton, the latest patent lawyer to get on the Institute dole. She was leaving; he was arriving. Hands were shaken. Hello. Nice to meet you. Gotta run to a meeting. But something about his manner stayed with her. Had he lingered too long at the door, or was there something in his body language? Business casual had become so pervasive, she could no longer decipher a handshake from an air kiss. His presence had been noted, without leaving a clear statement.

Jerome was calling, he claimed, because of a sore back. Being the head of Blackmore, one of the major investment/leveraged buyout firms, he could hardly be expected to sign up for a group Reformer class. The call also purported a need for information about setting up a total Pilates studio in his Park Avenue penthouse, and maybe in the Southampton place. Ostentatious? Perhaps. But his tone seemed too friendly for a money guy. Johanna racked her brain to try and remember what he was wearing when they met.

"Tell me all about the Pilates Chair," he said. "That design looks like someone other than just Joe was involved." She could hear the upturn in his voice. Maybe Pilates was a smokescreen, an excuse to call.

Probably she was reading too much into his tone. Rich, powerful American men in their fifties who are free from their starter wives usually want to go back to young women with very young eyes. Eyes that will see them as Mr. Wonderful or can't see through them the way an older woman's eyes can. Jerome's interest surprised her.

"Dick tells me Pilates is not just your business, but your secret as well," he said. "I figure those of us who have made it this far should stick together. So what do you say,

Johanna? Share your secrets over dinner at Per Se?"

"Sure, Jerome," she said. "But you'd better come with your own secrets to share."

"I'm an open book," he lied.

When they hung up, she googled him. All the right schools, clubs, charities, connections. And the fortune, which he'd made. Undoubtedly such a resume would have some great war stories. She wanted to hear them. Not just the successes, but the failures, too. Plus, hadn't he been smart enough to appear enigmatic? It had been a long time since she had found male rapport. Anglo men in Santa Fe weren't interested in women interested in business. Jerome might 'get' her ambitions, frustrations, and all. God, she could use a dose of that! Someone who understood the challenges.

And the revenge. After all, if the Wunda Chair now reborn as the Pilates Chair® succeeded—and with recent alliances it had a good shot—all the other apparatus manufacturers out there would be stuck with their Wunda relics. It would be just as if they had to use some old black, squat, rotary phones of yesterday while she would be using the lightest, sleekest, cell phone.

Standing Pilates time had come. The Institute's newest program was almost ready. She'd made sure to protect it and its patented suspension belt. Soon to be followed by a DVD and a book. And now *Diet Directives.* Anyone really involved in the body biz of today needed to cover both diet and fitness. Yet she was the only Pilates company with a diet program. Connecting the dots should be getting easier since they were practically on top of one another by now. Didn't anyone else see the collision?

She was eager to hear what someone like Jerome might have to say about the body biz. Pilates, since the trademark had been liberated, was now competing in the maistream fitness industry. It was no longer a business where you just had to answer the phone because the media exposure had sent you more business than you could handle. Now you had to compete for clients or to register the course or to ship the Reformer. Ten years ago, you hardly had to advertise. The Institute should have made a bundle by now. Whatever little they'd made had been shipped out to trademark owners, apparatus companies, and her own personal favorite, the legal profession. But hopefully, she could put her legal diatribes on hold. Meeting Jerome at her lawyer's office might be her first positive legal encounter.

It took her longer than usual to dress. She hadn't thrown this many knits on a bed in ages. She pulled off a Sonia Rykiel and tried on an old Alaia. She finally settled on a blood red Gaultier skin-tight jersey dress. Shoes? She had hated the dust and gravel that made heels so problematic in

Santa Fe. Hated the urban cowgirls sitting with their legs crossed and pointing out from under every restaurant table just to show off their brightly colored Tony Llamas. She was so glad to be back in a civilized society of level concrete and taxis. Never mind the dog shit, she had seen much worse. She went with the Manolos, took one final look, grabbed her keys, and headed out the door.

Jerome poured their first of glass of Petrus. He was slender and straight-shouldered in his tailored black jacket and crisp white shirt, his silver hair cropped short and neat.

"How does it work exactly?"

He was referring to the Diet Directives program. Per Se's sixteen tables were taken up with the New York elite who had to be seen at the latest eatery with the most impossible reservation. Luckily, The *New York Times* had affirmed the cuisine as sublime.

"It's easy," she said. "You count bites. An appropriate meal is 22 to 24 bites."

The waiter delivered their appetizer of seared foie gras with raspberry coulis.

"Watch," she said. This serving is only eight bites. Quality is expected here, not quantity, also foie gras is costly, and will be harder to find soon."

He nodded, "Let's enjoy it then. The bites sound right."

Choosing the small fork, he sliced through a silky corner of foie gras, brushed it through the swirl of raspberry then savored it.

"What happens if you are in a restaurant or at some charity affair?" he continued. "Suppose you lose track—if you're deep in conversation—or, I don't know, distracted by a beautiful woman sitting across from you?"

She slid her fork through the foie gras again. "Is this a common scenario for you? If it is you could keep track with one of those little golf clickers that I need to add up my too-numerous strokes. You probably have never used one."

As he sliced off another sliver of foie gras obviously pleased by her confidence in his golf game, her mind started churning.

"What?" he said. "You've got that look again."

This was their first date. Surely he hadn't identified her looks already.

"Don't act so surprised," he said. "One feverish mind always recognizes another. Spill it."

She put her fork down and had a sip of wine. "Well, getting back to my counting theory, I have been toying around with the idea of a kind of watch, a pedometer watch."

He furrowed his brow at her. "Go on, I think I'm tracking you."

"You know," she said. "You wear a pedometer at your waist and they keep track of how many steps you've taken. You walk ten thousand steps a day and you're thin!"

"Right." He laughed. "My sister had one. She walked, and walked around her house in Greenwich. My brother-in-law said she marched like a palace guard. He would come home from work and salute her."

"Did it work?"

He shook his head. "Saluting? Yeah, she started acting like a Marine, but never lost any weight. She'd hate you."

"So," he said. "Pedometer watches. Help me here, the connection?"

"Well," she said. But she was distracted, possibly interested.

Jerome was studying her. She liked that.

"I got it," he said quickly. "Your pause could not have been more gracious. A watch that keeps track of how many bites someone takes.... We might take that on."

"Is this how you made your fortune. Giving people what they want?"

She wrapped her fingers around her wrist and made a chewing motion. The waiter cleared the empty foie gras plate.

Then his furrowed brow smoothed. "You know watch sales were down ten percent last year."

Johanna nodded. "That doesn't surprise me. Who needs a watch any more? We all carry cell phones with the time right there."

"I have a friend at Swatch," he said. "I could put you in touch."

"In touch?" Johanna said.

His mouth spread slowly into a smile that was a hint crooked.

"What?" she said. "Now *you've* got that look."

The smile widened revealing straight white teeth. He picked up his wine glass and tilted it toward her. *"Salud,"* he said.

They leaned forward and let more than their glasses touch.

30

LEE

Subject: The Comeback Kid!
Date: July 19, 2006 1:40 PM
From: Lee Raney <Leeraney19@aol.com>
To: Johanna Breyers <Johanna@tmpilates.com >

Can I call you the Comeback Kid now? It's official right? The Pilates Chair sits atop the equipment charts? Sara— you remember her from our first video?—just came back from Vegas and the big Fitness show. She loved the Chair and all that goes with it: the workout, the music, the design. She said the Chair was the talk of the show. Trainers lined up to test drive it. All fabulous. Boy, I wish I could have been there to video it, especially with the grip you promised me. Remember? The days when we were starting out seem like another life time. Hey, don't you miss all those calls about the Pilots Method? Now, even Pharrell is rapping about Pilates stretching you out!

Seriously, how do you feel? Are you exhilarated, exhausted, both? And was it worth it? I mean I knew you'd never quit. But almost everyone else thought the Institute would fold, especially when the legal business kept us from using the name. I couldn't believe we had to black out the P word from all the encyclopedias we had printed just so we could use them and then beep it out whenever it came up on our video. Then, of course, we had to rework all the materials so we could float around his name and stay within the legal prescription. What a dose of eating crow!

Thanks for sending me the new books. *Standing Pilates* looks great. I told you your photo belonged on the cover. The exercises are challenging even for us old-timers. Only Eve would have been in perfect form the first time. She's probably doing them right now. Remember when she told us that Joe said his work was intended - and should - develop. I hate to think what would have happened if the trademark hadn't been cancelled. Now, there are so many directions in which the work can be taken.

Say hi to Meredith. We speak once a year for my annual bite check-up. I love it that I have a lifetime membership on the Diet Directives site. When I'm in the chat room, my experience helps newer members. Remember when I came for that first and only interview? I mean it was really, really weird. I never expected I would get in on the ground floor of the best body methods ever. You told me when were walking—it was like running for me then—how lucky you had been to find Pilates in your twenties before you damaged your bod with nutsy routines. I expect that 50 years from now I'll still be telling the story of that first afternoon when I saw those contraptions. And, the picture of Joe in his shorts. I'm saving it all for my memoir. Speaking of my life's work, my show at Santa Fe Site did well. Sold ten paintings the first weekend. You were right again: you have to do the time to succeed. I've almost forgotten how many times I was ready to give up.

I know you aren't hurrying back here any time soon, so our next get together will have to be in the Big Apple. While seeing you is a major motivator for the trip East, it's not the only one. I'm trying for a New York show. Think I'm aiming too high? Just kidding. I know you've always believed I could accomplish anything I truly aimed for. Thanks to you, I now believe it too.

See you soon.

Lee

Image courtesy of Peak Pilates